BROTHER HOOD

JANET McDONALD

BROTHER HOOD

Frances Foster Books   Farrar, Straus and Giroux / New York

www.fsgkidsbooks.com

Library of Congress Cataloging-in-Publication Data
McDonald, Janet, 1953–
    Brother hood / Janet McDonald.— 1st ed.
        p.   cm.
    Summary: Sixteen-year-old Nate, an academically gifted student who
attends an exclusive private boarding school, straddles two cultures as he
returns home for occasional visits to see his family and "gangsta crew" in
Harlem, New York.
    ISBN 0-374-30995-7
    [1. Gifted children—Fiction.   2. African Americans—Fiction.
3. Boarding schools—Fiction.   4. Schools—Fiction.   5. Harlem (New
York, N.Y.)—Fiction.]   I. Title.

PZ7.M4784178Br 2004
[Fic]—dc22

                                                        2003060670

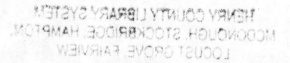

To readers who take the risk of stepping with a book
from the confines of their day
into the adventure of their lives

Acknowledgments

With thanks to my editor, Frances Foster, who mercilessly raises the bar and constantly makes me laugh; to her indomitable assistant, Janine O'Malley; and to my agent, Charlotte Sheedy, who perseveres, always. I am especially grateful to my brother Kevin, who waited for me, and to Paulette Constantino, Annie Gleason, Lisa Hayes, and Janet Prata, who waited with me.

BROTHER HOOD

The high-speed train raced towards the city through woods of poplar and pine, passing local stations, fenced yards, brick houses, and distant, lean horses that vanished from view almost as soon as they came into focus. On a typical Friday afternoon it would be transporting graying professors rustling through papers, restless sales reps negotiating on cell phones, and tired domestics staring out the windows. But on this day, which marked the beginning of a weekend break, the train was bustling with students from the private schools and elite colleges tucked away in the slopes of Edessa Hills, a wealthy community north of Manhattan.

"All tickets, please," called the conductor. "Have your tickets ready."

He reached the last row of the car and repeated himself. The passenger didn't respond. Bent over his book, he was aware of nothing but a panicked Raskolnikov crouched behind a door with noises on the stairwell and bodies a few feet away from him on the floor. The young man had close-cropped hair and was wearing a freshly ironed white dress shirt, a tan tie, black slacks, and the obligatory black blazer with the Fletcher School crest emblazoned on the breast pocket.

"Ticket . . . please."

Nathaniel Whitely jumped, then handed over his ticket. He had been engrossed in the novel they were reading in his literature classics course.

The conductor punched two little holes in the student's ticket and moved into the next car calling, "Tickets! Your tickets, please!"

A blond head popped up over the seat in front of Nathaniel's. It belonged to Spencer Adams, the lacrosse team's goalkeeper, and the younger student's mentor and French tutor. His school blazer swung from a window hook. The hazel Izod dress shirt he was wearing was nicely laundered, the black Brooks Brothers tie was silk, and the Cottonport twill khakis were perfectly crisp.

"Oh, *that's* what you're doing. I was wondering why the guy had to keep asking for your ticket. What's got you hypnotized?"

Nathaniel held his place with his finger. *"Crime and Punishment.* This guy Raskolnikov, a *law student* no less, killed two old women for money, then somebody shows up outside their *unlocked* door while he's still inside. He barely manages to get the latch on in time. That's where I was when the conductor appeared. I'm sweating through my shirt. What's crazy is that he did it mostly to prove to himself he could get away with it—you know, the perfect murder kind of thing. That's sick."

"I loved that book, even though the guy's a jerk. At least he's more interesting than Holden Caulfield, whom you'll get to know and loathe if you take sociology next year. He's the main character in *Catcher in the Rye*, this whiny, shallow boy with major hostility issues and an unwarranted superiority complex. You're supposed to feel sorry that he's alienated and lonely, but he's so obnoxious you want *him* to end up in the Central Park lake with the ducks he's so worried about. If I carried on like him, you know what my dad would do to me?"

"Yep. You've told me a hundred times."

"Heir today, gone tomorrow," they both said at once, laughing so hard a couple of passengers couldn't help but smile.

Adams Global Electronics, a major manufacturer of electronic products, had provided two generations of the Adams clan with the kind of sumptuous lifestyle that only the most monied white Anglo-Saxon Protestant moguls could buy. Private jets flew the family to European capitals, where they stayed in homes they actually owned. A small army of domestic staff ensured that none of the children would ever learn to cook a meal, clean a room, or fix a broken toy. As if a room with video games, a DVD player, two digital video cameras, a flat-screen TV, and a luxury cell phone with MP3 player, photo caller ID, and a stereo earpiece weren't enough, Spencer not only was already guaranteed a spot at Harvard, he was also due to inherit a fortune on his twenty-first birthday.

The train heaved to a stop. Commuters in light coats carried computer cases and lugged shopping bags through the aisles. The man who'd been asleep next to Nathaniel opened his eyes suddenly as if an alarm had gone off, snatched his briefcase from the overhead rack, and hurried to the door. Spencer hopped into the empty seat.

"Look out that window, Nathaniel. See those cool cars parked over there, Alfa Romeos, Benzes, Jaguars? See those lovely ladies inside waiting for their husbands? See those three-story colonials in the distant bucolic hills? And the bright sun beaming down approvingly on it all? That's our future you're looking at. My ancestors founded this country, yours built it, albeit against their will and for that I offer my *profoundest* apologies. But today, in this moment, you're what, sixteen?, and I'm seventeen. Cool. Today our destiny is one—shaped by Fletcher, honed at Harvard, and released on the world to rule!"

"Yeah, right. You're tripping like that megalomaniac Raskolnikov. And anyway, I want a Hummer. Silver-gray."

"Hummers are tacky. And Raskolnikov's a loser. A broke Russian peasant turned failed law student who knocks off a couple of defenseless old broads for a handful of rubles, then freaks out and confesses. Violence doesn't make you superior, it makes you common. Everyone's violent. It's boring. We are decidedly *not* common. We are Fletcher Falcons! And like golden *flèches* we shoot straight to the bull's-eye."

"Maybe *your* flesh is golden, Adams . . . Mine is black."

"*Flèche*, Nathaniel, *flèche*. How are you gonna learn French if you won't study the vocabulary words I give you?!"

Nathaniel laughed. "Oh, you mean *flèche*, as in *arrow*."

Spencer Adams and Nathaniel Whitely rode into Grand Central Terminal, the one chatting on his cell, the other reading. The world they shared abruptly split apart the moment the train came to a stop. They shook hands and said, "See ya." Spencer hurried towards the taxi-stand exit. Nathaniel headed in the opposite direction. It was funny, he and Spencer had become friends right away when he first arrived at Fletcher as a freshman. And they both lived in New York, but neither had ever invited the other to his home. It just never came up, as if they had an understanding, an unspoken agreement.

When Nathaniel was sure he'd blurred into the rush-hour throng, he stopped and waited at the four-faced clock. A young woman with long black hair and a cashmere coat asked him how to get to the concourse photo exhibition. He said he didn't know. She smiled. Thanks anyway. A police officer on foot patrol nodded at him. Nathaniel returned the nod. An old man breathing hard tapped Nathaniel's arm. How the hell, he wanted to know, did one get out of this place? Nathaniel showed him to the nearest exit and scanned the vast terminal. Spencer was long gone, maybe already at his parents' East 86th Street town house. Confident he wouldn't be seen, Nathaniel took the ramp to the lower level, his crammed knapsack slung over his shoulder, and headed to the men's room.

Moments later, he strolled out of the men's room and made his way through the long, busy corridors that led to the Times Square–bound shuttle. Now he was met with nervous looks and wary glances from some—most simply stared straight ahead. As if they weren't scrutinizing him. As if they weren't measuring the potential threat. As if from the corners of their eyes they weren't keenly aware of every move of the homeboy. The Fletcher School student had stripped off the private-school uniform and donned full urban regalia. Precariously low denim jeans dangled off his hips underneath an oversized black sweatshirt and red leather bomber. A white nylon do-rag hung like a blond mane from beneath a black cap turned slightly to the side. As a final touch, he'd put on a pair of Police brand shades.

Waiting on the packed platform of the IRT uptown number 2 train, Nathaniel smiled to himself at the empty space left around him and the other young black guys waiting, a circle outside of which safely stood the other straphangers. A crowded train squealed to a stop. Those eager to push their way into the cars eyed those desperate to get out. The doors opened and a chaos of intimacy ensued as the two groups shoved, squeezed, and slid against each other. Nathaniel liked the forced closeness of the subway, the way it made people say polite things like "Excuse me" and "Oops, sorry," even *if* purely out of fear.

Packed in as they were, the passengers had no

personal space to jealously guard, only their simple, vulnerable humanity seeking respect. And no one respected it more than Nathaniel. Maybe that trait came from the way his parents had raised him and his brother—to look out for each other and for their friends and neighbors as well. On the subway, if he saw an old person or a little kid or a girl getting crushed, he'd use his body like a barrier to keep a cushion of space around them. They rarely noticed but it made him feel good to do it.

The subway train roared through the dark tunnel, snips of colorful tags and graffiti art flitting by like images in a child's cartoon flipbook. Riders leaned against doors marked DO NOT LEAN or grasped the overhead handles, swaying with the car's movement. People reading newspapers artfully unfolded a half page at a time. Those lucky enough to be sitting closed their eyes or stole looks at whoever wasn't looking at them. Some read books, glancing with irritation at neighbors listening to music so loud it blasted from their headphones. The space above the sooty windows was papered with ads in English and Spanish touting every completely safe procedure, incredible opportunity, and low-cost service from affordable cosmetic surgery to accredited business schools specializing in the careers of tomorrow to lawyers to call immediately in case of an accident in the workplace.

When the train at last reached his stop, it was full of black and brown folks traveling to Harlem and on to the Bronx. The only white riders left were a scattering of Columbia University students drawn to cheap uptown housing. Maneuvering through the crowd, Nathaniel took the steps two at a time and came out onto 125th Street in the heart of Harlem, USA.

Nate made his way up the thoroughfare he'd always known as Malcolm X Boulevard but which his father called Lenox Avenue. A row of five-story redstones reflected the fiery glint of the evening sun. Dusk was settling across Harlem, a place that shared only a name with the wealthy white village Peter Stuyvesant established centuries ago in honor of the Dutch city of Haarlem. With scores of clubs and lounges, countless churches and restaurants, busloads of tourists and a world of history all crammed into one neighborhood, Harlem was as often the flourishing metropolis it seemed to be as it was the troubled urban zone of legend.

Traffic was backed up as usual and drivers leaned on their horns, frantic to get to whatever Friday night party, dinner, movie, b-ball game, or date they'd lined up for the evening. Jaywalking pedestrians weaved their way through the tangled mass of city buses, airport shuttles, delivery trucks, and passenger cars. Angry shouts and blasting hip-hop competed with the furious honking of vehicles. Spoiled by his quiet campus, Nate covered his ears, darted across the avenue, and turned down 128th Street. At that moment it hit him. He was home and, like him, home was changing. Everywhere were signs of Harlem's gentrification or renaissance, depending on who was doing the looking. Nate saw refurbished buildings where once stood dilapidated drug dens. He noticed tidy, spacious supermarkets in the place of overpriced, dirty bodegas. But what he noticed most were the Asian, African, and white faces of Harlem's newest residents. Yes, Harlem had come a long way. And so had he.

Nate was a seventh grader when he came to the attention of SOAR, Columbia University's Student Outreach and Recruitment initiative. Designed to spot promising public school students with the potential to thrive at prestigious private schools, the program had an impressive roster of success stories, including astronaut Jan Prata, brain surgeon Dr. Liz Brown, and music mogul Nat Bryer of Dion Records.

Columbia adviser Randall Stone first met with the

school guidance counselor to confirm Nate's academics and class conduct before sitting down with the boy's mother and father. The Whitelys were proud of their son but worried about his leaving a familiar neighborhood to attend some school for rich white kids who might be prejudiced or hostile or just stuck-up. As well adjusted as they knew Nate to be, they felt uneasy.

Randall, himself a product of the program and a graduate of Fletcher, assured the Whitelys that SOAR students were well counseled before their private school sojourn, that academic support was made available throughout their stay, and that Fletcher had a peer mentor system that helped new students get oriented and permitted them to develop friendships from day one. The school was located in a safe and quiet town in Clinton County, home to some of the highest tax brackets in the country.

Still his parents worried. Such a dramatic acceleration in Nate's schooling might completely demoralize his brother, Eli, who was struggling to keep up with the rest of his class. Randall was adamant—they shouldn't stunt the development of one child to shield the feelings of the other. Nate *needed* this opportunity, he *deserved* it, and it would be *just plain wrong* to deprive a black child of tools that would enable him to pry open the doors of his small universe and soar forth. Mr. and

Mrs. Whitely decided that if this was what *Nate* wanted, he had their blessing. Nate wanted it.

Making his way down the street, Nate smiled to himself, proud to be back home in Harlem, a Fletcher student. That thought always made him smile. All of a sudden he noticed the group of guys heading towards him. He caught his breath and braced his body for whatever was to come. Only a half block away from his front door and pretty quick on his legs, he could run for it. Should he try to holler for Eli? For his father? There wasn't time.

The boys, sporting black do-rags and bombers, encircled him.

" 'Sup wichoo, you got a problem?" asked one, scanning Nate from behind dark shades.

Nate knew he better not let it show he was scared.

"Nah, dawg," said Nate.

"Dawg?" sneered the guy, stepping forward. "I ain'tcha dawg . . ."

At that moment another one appeared and walked up to Nate.

"Yo, *whatda*?? . . ." this one asked angrily, then stopped. He squinted. "Nate? Nate! Awww *man*, it's *Schoolie*, ya dumb suckers!"

The tension fell like a theater curtain.

"Ha, ha, Schoolie! We was just messin' wicha," said Ride, laughing.

"*Wassuuup?!*" cheered Double Fo'.

"That's Schoolie?" said Hydro, looking over the top of his glasses and pretending not to have recognized Nate. "Man, you was *that* close to gettin' dropped!"

The friends exchanged one-shouldered hugs and bumped fists.

"I knew it was y'all," lied Nate. "Anybody'd recognize Hustle's wanksta walk."

Eric Samson, called "Hustle" because of his entrepreneurial ways, and Nate, called "Schoolie" because of his affinity for school, had grown up on the same street and gone to the same elementary school. Both excelled in the early grades, but Nate soon surpassed his friend, who seemed to lose interest in school when his parents split up and went their separate ways, leaving him to fend for himself. First his attendance suffered, then his grades, then any kid who crossed his path, and finally half of Harlem, as the hulking teenager made it his goal to "bring pain to the lame." He lived wherever his friends let him crash and hadn't seen his parents in a couple of years. The two boys sat on the top step of a brownstone while the others wandered off down the street.

"So what's the deal, Hustle, what you into besides block patrol?"

"You know me, man, I *stays* busy. Got a couple of shorties round the way."

"I don't know *how* you manage that harem thing."

"Hey . . ." Hustle laughed proudly. "That's not my *whole* life. I'm doing a little this, a little that, some boosting . . . Lemme know if you need any clothes . . . Muscle jobs for dealers that got beefs with the competition." He paused. "But don't worry, I don't let *none* of them vultures come on *our* block. I'm just out here, you know how we roll up here in Harlem." He punched Nate's shoulder. "You need to hook up with the Brotherhood, Schoolie, these streets got all the schooling you need. And you get paid right away, ain't about waiting for four years like y'all college boys. Check out my ice, check out my gold."

Nate examined Hustle's flashing diamond rings and glitzy Rolex watch. He noticed the time.

"Whoa!" He leapt to his feet. "I gotta go, my folks are waiting for me. I'll check you later."

"Ah-ight, my man, holla atcha tomorrow!" said Hustle.

Nate ran down the block.

Mrs. Whitely heard the key turn in the lock.

"Nate! It's about time! Did you walk from upstate?" She threw her arms around her son.

"Let the boy put his bag down at least, Deena," called

17

Mr. Whitely from the kitchen, where he was frying up some catfish.

"A mother's gotta welcome her child, Jared."

"But not tackle him," said Mr. Whitely, laughing. "How was the ride in, son?"

"Okay," Nate managed to say, squeezed tight against his heavyset mother. She liked to boast that he inherited his brains from her because from as far back as he could remember she was always reading—to him or to herself. Comic strips, magazines, even her home health care attendant study guides.

"Where's Eli, Ma? He betta be home to kick it with his little bro."

"Eliiiii! Your brother's home!" sang Mrs. Whitely, her voice filling the cramped two-bedroom apartment the family had shared for two decades. At thirty-eight she could still be playful as a teenager when she was happy.

A commotion of banging doors and heavy footsteps announced Eli.

The same height but leaner than Nate, Eli was as handsome as his brother. His eyes were darker, as if holding secrets in shadow. They both had the full lips and strong chin of their mother and the broad shoulders of their father. But the younger boy was thicker, more solidly built. And a better student. Eli had dropped out of high school.

"Wassup," said Eli. "Gimme some love, young'n."

The brothers slapped hands.

"Whoa, I see you trying to get your swell on." Eli poked Nate's bicep again and again like a shopper testing a grapefruit. "What sports they got you doin' up there?"

"Lacrosse."

"Lacrosse?! What's that? Y'all schoolboys need to be playing some ball, some *b*-ball." He did an imaginary fadeaway jumper.

Mr. Whitely walked up to them, wiping his wet hands on a plaid cloth. He gave his son a bear hug and some hard slaps on the back.

"So . . . school good? You're on your way to being a college man!"

A small paunch now covered the washboard abs Mr. Whitely used to flex onstage during his days as a competitive bodybuilder, but he was quite fit and athletic for a man of forty. A lifelong love affair with cars had led him to a job as an auto mechanic. Twenty years later he was still repairing engines and was in line to take over Harlem River Auto when the owner, Ed Burghardt, retired.

"Something smells *gooood*," said Nate, taking off his jacket and cap. "Let's eat."

"I hear *that*," said Eli.

"Well, since I caught, killed, scaled, and cooked the

thing," said Mr. Whitely, "maybe the lady of the house can serve it?"

"That's a deal. But I'm not washing dishes." She looked at Nate.

"Hey, I'm a weary traveler."

Everyone looked at Eli.

"Why I always gots to do dishes, wassup widdat?"

"Because you always *gots* to eat," answered Mr. Whitely.

Eli needed to learn responsibility, his parents often complained. He was getting too old to be lazing around the house and hanging out. He'd respond that there wasn't squat out in the job market for a dropout. Mr. Whitely had persuaded old Burghardt to hire Eli at the car shop, but Eli wouldn't accept a regular work schedule. He had to stay freed up, he said, to look for a job. As his parents' patience wore thin, the family fights grew louder until everyone simply avoided the topic.

Eli changed the subject. "So, Nate, Shantay know you home?" Nate was going to surprise his girlfriend.

"Nah, but she will."

Mr. Whitely cleared his throat. "Just be responsible. Like I always tell you boys, if the girl gets in trouble, you in *more* trouble."

"Not *always*," said Eli, the father of three children who didn't even know his name. "This a free country and that old school style of tying down a young brother—man, that's played out."

Both his parents glared at him but didn't say a word. Nate was home and his weekend would *not* be ruined with arguing and fighting.

"I hear you, Dad," said Nate, suddenly serious.

The differences between the brothers were most noticeable in school. As a student, Nate was the opposite of his brother. A fast and natural learner, he loved books and delighted in the attention his high reading scores got him. Not only did they make *him* look good, they made his *teachers* look even better. A star like Nate cast a flattering light on them all, and for that, they loved him. They couldn't give him enough A's on his tests. They couldn't pen enough superlatives on his report cards. They couldn't praise him enough when his mother showed up for Open School Week.

While other bright kids found themselves mocked, teased, and sometimes even beaten up by jealous classmates, Nate had no such problems. To begin with, he was built like his father, who as a young man had come in second in the Mr. Empire State bodybuilding competition.

But what really kept the others from harassing him the way they did other kids in the gifted students program was this—they liked him. He was neither rudely conceited nor falsely humble. He didn't act weird or keep to himself. He had no high-water pants or brand X sneakers. He didn't go around acting special. And why would he? Nate didn't *feel* special or even different for that matter. He just felt happy reading. It offered intense experiences and exciting adventures all in the safety of the room he shared with Eli, who hated books.

The way he saw it, he was simply doing what he enjoyed. The same way his friends enjoyed playing video games or learning new dances or hanging out. The same way Eli enjoyed taking things from stores without paying for them. Girls found Nate cute. Boys chose him to shoot hoops with. And everybody forgave him for being smart and even forgot that he was number one in the school district.

Nate and his mother went into the kitchen to prepare the plates.

"Where's your snazzy little outfit from school?" she asked. "You never wear it home and it looks so good on you."

"In my bag. Can you see me strutting around *here* in it? It's strictly for school. School's school, the hood's the hood, and it's all good."

Mrs. Whitely shook her head. "Just listen to *you*. You sound like a hoodie instead of a preppie."

He started bopping around the kitchen. "That's word, shorty. I'm the preppie hoodie comin' atcha live from the Apollo!"

She laughed, scooping greens and candied yams onto four plates while Nate talked about his school friends, favorite teachers, and best classes.

"You seeing Randall while you're here?" she asked. "Once in a while I'll get a call from him asking about you. He lives up in Sugar Hill now. I think he's working in advertising or architecture. I don't know, something with an *a*."

"Mmmm, let's see . . . What could it be? Acupuncture? Airport security? Acrobatics?"

She pulled his ear.

"Astrology?"

She pulled it again.

"I know! Aromatherapy!"

"All right, Mr. Wiseguy! Whatever he's doing, he's making good money. And he's your friend."

"Mr. Stone's my adviser, Ma, not a friend."

"Adviser, friend, whatever you wanna call him, he looks out for you. You just make sure you call him while you're in town."

Having lived in the neighborhood when black professionals like Randall never would've settled north of 96th Street, Deena Whitely liked the changes that were

happening in Harlem. When the newly married Whitelys moved from a Brooklyn tenement to Manhattan, she
thought the good times had at last arrived. Harlem was
back. Glossy magazine photos of row houses with fine
brickwork, bay windows, and elaborate metalwork
proclaimed it. Breathless reporters walking TV crews
through Harlem's last freestanding mansions declared
it. And real estate developers packaged and sold it to
yuppies and buppies from all over the country.

It seemed like everyone who could qualify for a bank
loan was scrambling to buy something, anything, in
Harlem. They flocked to areas like Hamilton Heights
with its spacious turn-of-the-century houses, fine apart-
ments, and huge Romanesque-style homes; to Strivers
Row with its car parks behind every house; and to
Mount Morris Park, with its brownstone, limestone,
and terra-cotta brick town houses. If shut out there,
they snatched up any property above 110th Street. They
all yearned to live with the ghosts of Harlem residents.
Dr. May Chinn. Ralph Ellison. Billie Holiday. James
Baldwin. Even Harry Houdini.

The Whitelys' combined income was a child's al-
lowance compared to the salary of a single Wall Street
lawyer, so they settled for a small rental apartment on a
side street. They would just have to work hard and save
as much as they could. The important thing was they'd

gotten in on the ground level. But that's exactly where they stayed. As the hype grew, so did the prices. Then it all stalled. Harlem's perpetual renaissance got caught in a permanent tangle of urban undertow. And all the magazines in the world couldn't airbrush away the neighborhood's underlying poverty, drugs, and crime. But things were once again changing for the better, and Mrs. Whitely hoped that by the time Nate was a professional, he'd also choose to stay uptown.

That night, Nate sleepily dumped the contents of his knapsack in a corner of the bedroom he shared with Eli. Out dropped the Dostoyevsky novel, his rolled-up Fletcher clothes, a shoe with his tie stuck in it, a cell phone, toothbrush, pocket-sized mirror, looseleaf notebook, an underground hip-hop compilation, another shoe, and a new package of condoms. He sprawled back on the bed with his cell, staring at the ceiling. Home. One day he'd move his folks out of this peeling, run-down apartment and into one of those nice houses over in Morris Park with the stained-glass windows. But first there was Fletcher to finish, then college, then a job. He'd do it though. They deserved it. He flipped over, propped himself up on his elbows, and checked the clock on the cell. Not too late. He pressed Speed Dial.

This Shantay. Wassup? If you calling me, must be you wanna talk to me. 'Nuff said.

He waited for the beep. Where was she this late on a Friday night? He should've called earlier.

"Hey, it's me. Where you at? I meant to call before I left school, but everything got mad rushed. I'm home for the weekend. Holla." He hesitated before pushing End. "I miss you, girl."

Hustle often teased him about being too soft with the shorties, warned him they'd play him for a fool, but what the hell, he *did* miss her. He clicked off the light switch and slid in under the covers. Eli's bed was empty.

Nate woke up early, just as he did at school. He'd slept so deeply that when he tried to open his eyes he almost couldn't. They felt glued shut. He sat up and blinked the clock into focus. Then he dressed, eased down the hall, and slipped out the front door.

Unlike Nate, Harlem was awakening not with a yawn and a stretch but with the pizzazz of a Miles Davis improvisation and the pirouettes of a freestyle rapper. Up and down 125th Street the neighborhood buzzed with energy. African women in colorful dresses and head wraps looked his way, then whispered and smiled. He watched them raise the gates on their hair-braiding salons barely as large as a socialite's walk-in closet and chuckled at the joke his mother liked to make about Africans coming to Harlem to find the *real* motherland.

Kids his age with jobs at checkout counters and in

department store stockrooms milled around security gates, waiting to begin work. He thought about how they spent their days and was glad to still be in school. There seemed to be more East Asians than he remembered, he thought as he entered one of the many fast-food doughnut shops they owned. Harlem had certainly changed a lot from when he was little and it was pretty much exclusively black American. Now there were almost as many Chinese restaurants as soul food places, and tourists were everywhere. He finished his honey-dipped doughnut as he passed a tour group posing for cameras beneath the Apollo Theater marquee.

"Say *cheeeeese*," he called out, making them all laugh just in time for the shot.

The neighborhood seemed a little different with each visit back, but overall it was still his hood and definitely all good. He walked back home feeling energized and opened the door to the sounds of the television, the washing machine, and his mother's coffee grinder.

"Morning, Ma."

Mrs. Whitely was in an unusual place, the kitchen. Nate kissed her cheek.

"Good morning! You're up and out bright and early. I thought you were still getting your beauty sleep. I was just fixing you something to eat. I hope you got me my paper."

"Oops."

"Oops? I'll give you *oops* . . . upside your head. You know I need my daily newspaper." She cracked an egg open on the side of a bowl. "Go back there and see if Eli made it home."

Nate checked the bedroom and returned to the kitchen.

"Nah," he said. "Shantay call?"

"No, not this morning. How many eggs you want?"

Just then the doorbell rang. Nate opened the door and there stood Hustle in an extravagant powder blue Sean Jean microfleece full-zip hoody set he'd lifted from a trendy midtown store. He had a newspaper folded under his arm.

" 'Sup, Schoolie?"

"Nice warm-up suit," responded Nate. "Hey, you done with the newspaper? My moms needs it."

"*Hell no*, I ain't done with this paper I *just bought* to check if my number hit. Now, if she wanna *buy* it off me, maybe we can talk. That's fitty cent for the paper itself, plus fitty cent for me going through the trouble of gettin' it, so that's a total of . . ."

"Yo, *Fitty Cent*, it's *not* ya birthday. Now, get up off the newspaper before—"

Mrs. Whitely called from the kitchen. "Who is it, Nate? Eli back?"

"No, Ma, it's some MC Hammer–looking hoodlum!"

Hustle greeted Mrs. Whitely at the stove. "G'morning, Moms. It sure smells good in here. I picked up the paper for you on my way over."

"Thank you, Eric!" She glanced at Nate, who was rolling his eyes. "Can I offer you some breakfast?"

The boys sat down to eggs, bacon, and talk about girls. Mrs. Whitely went to check the load in the washing machine.

Hustle lowered his voice. "Man, don't sweat Shantay not answering her phone last night. I got a girl already lined up for you."

"I ain't sweating, I'm eating," answered Nate. "Shantay and me tight. It's cool."

"Well, your face look more tight than cool. Anyway, we hangin' today, right? Got some . . . items to show you. Peep this." Hustle pulled a sparkling gold watch from his pocket. "This ain't no . . . what they say in that movie *Donnie Brasco*? *Fugazy*. This ain't no fugazy, Schoolie. This the real deal. It's yours if you want it 'cause you my boy. I'll give you a really good price."

Things were moving just a little too fast for Nate. His mind was still back on the Shantay topic. "I *have* a watch."

"That ain't a *watch*. It's a Timex. A wackex."

Nate laughed. "Wackex. *You* a wackex. It tells time and that's all I need. Now can I eat, Mr. Traveling Salesman?"

"Hey, I'ma *get* my hustle on. Check it out, I came across some merchandise last weekend. Phat Farm, Rocawear, Projectboy, Sean Jean, Ghetto Fabwear, FUBU . . . Got *all* they gear . . . leather jackets, oxford denim, nylon reversible, fleece. Jeans, jerseys, all kinda hats . . . them monk hats, the velour bucket like what Jay-Z wear . . . caps, headbands, visors . . . Come over, see for yourself. Cheap, too. They all rich as *mofos* and they gon' charge *us* mad cash for jeans. I don't care *who* name be on it, no pair of jeans should be costing hundreds."

Nate was amazed. "How you be boosting so *much* stuff? Don't clothes have them big clamps on 'em that trigger the alarms? Man, if you get busted with all that—"

"I'm a po*fess*ional, not no young boy stickin' a do-rag under his jacket. Now, if you wanna get something sexy for Shantay, the Baby Phat bustier and the Projectgirl mesh thong are *kickin'*!"

"*What's* kickin'?" asked Mrs. Whitely, suddenly reappearing, her white health-care-attendant uniform stretched tight across her bosom.

The boys "umm-ed" and "uhh-ed."

She pulled her coat from the hook behind the door.

"Uh-huh, just what I thought. Listen, Nate, I have a client this afternoon over on Riverside Drive, but I'll be back around six. I *hope*. This lady gets real clingy when it's time for me to go. So have fun, kids, and be careful." She felt in her pocket for her keys. "And when Eli comes in, tell him he *could've* called."

The door banged shut. Ever since somebody'd tried to jimmy it open, it wouldn't close without a hard yank. Hustle leaned towards Nate as if to stop anyone from hearing him.

"You know he pushin' a little rock and runnin' numbers now, right?"

"Who?"

"*Eli*. Your brother."

Nate dropped back against his chair and exhaled hard like he was blowing out a candle. "Wow."

Hustle agreed. "I ain't hatin' on your brother, but his thing is wak. He be takin' bets on foreigners' turf. And them hoodlums don't *play*, man. They ain't got values like us. They'll call in the Cleaners in a minute and tell 'em to pop ya grandma *first*, then go after you."

As far back as Nate could remember, Eli was messing up. First there was school. He flunked tests. He cut classes. He played hooky. He shoplifted. Their mother pleaded and cried. Their father shouted and punished. Nate offered to help him with his reading, check his algebra. Eli's answer was to drop out. He was in the tenth grade. Then girls began calling the house, sometimes crying, most times yelling, always with a baby bawling in the background. A baby they said was Eli's. The weekend before Nate's orientation visit to Fletcher, Eli came home one night beaten and bruised. He said he'd been mugged, but the family found out later that he'd been jumped by the father of one of his girlfriends.

So what *was* Eli's problem? Jealousy because he was always outshone? Insecurity because he failed the few times he *did* try? Cowardice because he lacked courage enough to face his flaws and grow his virtues? Or was it simple laziness born of years of receiving food, clothing, and shelter without having to lift a finger? Nate couldn't decipher Eli's issue; he just wanted him to work it out.

"If he gets my folks hurt . . ." Nate stared out the window. "The thing with Eli is, if you try to talk to him he gets all loud, saying you showing him disrespect. You think I should say something?"

Hustle rose from his chair. "I dunno, I dunno. Family feuds . . . that ain't the game I'm in. Hey, I tell ya this much though:

"The Brotherhood got the block / dead under lock
Fools bring they drama / we spray the Glock.

Punks betta learn / leave the one-two-eight alone
Or they end up in a urn / all ashes, dust and bone."

He did a self-congratulatory dance around the table. Nate cracked up.

"That was all right, Hustle!" he said, laughing. "But you can't battle the underground—Jin, Tonedeff, Black-alicious, Rakim . . ."

"Lemme take ya to school, Schoolie," said Hustle in a staccato rat-a-tat-tat. "I spit flava, the slaya of fake playas, my freestyle raw not wild, punks like Osama scream for Mama when I jet on the set, no frontin', gruntin', dog barkin', that's for the pound, I'm knockin' 'em down, shockin', rockin', knee-droppin' 'em to the ground . . . And that's just lesson one from the one and only Number One, my son. Big up Harlem, one love, I'm out."

"That's why you on the telly wid Justin and Nelly," Nate howled.

Hustle smacked his head. "Now *that* was wak. For somebody s'pose to be a child pedigree or whatever, you still a dumb ass. Go put some real clothes on, fool, so we can get this party *started.*"

While Nate was in the bedroom checking to see if his Phat Farm classic flava jeans looked right with Eli's Projectboy denim jacket, the front door swung open, making Hustle jump up and reach for something in the small of his back.

Eli strolled in, his eyes pink from partying. " 'Sup."

Hustle looked him up and down. " 'Sup."

Eli opened the refrigerator, sucked his teeth, and closed it. "Where da food?"

He walked to the bedroom and found Nate dressing.

"Hey Eli, you finally made it. Moms said you coulda called."

"That my jacket?"

Nate pretended not to hear the question. "What happened to your neck?"

Eli grinned as he examined the marks on his neck in the mirror. "Heat rash."

"Take it easy, Eli. Me and Hustle hitting the strip."

The sun had burned off the morning chill and it felt more like summer than autumn on the streets. They stepped off the block and onto Malcolm X Boulevard. Girls dressed in tight low-rider jeans turned their heads one way and their eyes the other as they stole looks at the two boys. Their flirtatious sway reminded Nate that Shantay still hadn't called. Hustle suggested they hit Mount Morris Park, where he and the Brotherhood dominated the benches and courts. Nate told Hustle how his school was in the middle of acres of green hills and it was like living in a gigantic park. What he wanted right then was the pavement, glass and steel, and brick and concrete of his urban world. Besides, he had to make a stop at the Schomburg.

"Come on!" protested Hustle. "You goin' to the *li*berry?!"

"It's not the library," claimed Nate, even though he knew better. "It's a black-culture center. I'm not stayin', I just have to look up something for school."

Hustle sucked his teeth and pouted all the way there. He insisted on waiting outside, not wanting to "be played" by nerds eyeballing him like he didn't belong in there.

The Schomburg Center for Research in Black Culture was indeed a library, with an enormous collection of African and African-American rare documents, books, and art. Mrs. Quilly, the librarian, had been there forever and had stories about everyone, from the young Colin Powell to author James Baldwin to sculptor Elizabeth Catlett. But what she most loved was when ordinary people and kids from the community took advantage of what she called "the treasure in their midst." Her face was radiant as she looked up at one kid she recognized very well.

"Nathaniel Whitely!" She lowered her head and looked over the top of her half-glasses. "Child!"

The slight woman with the blue-gray curls and thick stockings came around to the front of the information desk. She hugged him so hard heat rose into his ears.

"I'm *so* proud of you. Why, just yesterday I was telling someone about you, the smart little boy who used to *live* at the Schomburg and went off to an *exclusive* private school, thanks to his love of books and learning. These other young folks still running around with their drawers sticking out the top of their pants, greeting each other with the N-word. Used to be, a proud black man would deck *anyone* calling him that. Nowadays, these knuckleheads think it means hello."

She shook her head in dismay, then brightened again. "You're the living proof of what Harlemites can achieve."

Embarrassed and pleased at the same time, Nate quickly explained how he'd seen what looked like a church for Ethiopian Hebrews near his house. It sounded like they were black Jews, but he knew that wasn't possible. He was *really* curious and thought he might do a paper for school. Doing what she was famous for, Mrs. Quilly knew exactly where to direct him, and within a short while Nate had photocopied the basic information needed for the research he'd continue at school. He said goodbye to the librarian and hurried out as she seemed to be gearing up for another round of praise.

"That him?" asked the girl, her eyes carefully examining Nate as he stepped from the library. "Yeah, he *do* look good." She sidled up to him. "Hi, Schoolie. I'm Kyretha but I go by Ky for short. Why they call you Schoolie? Hustle said he real big in rap. He rap?"

Who was this *baby* Hustle had picked up? She couldn't have been older than thirteen. Nate didn't see even the bud of a breast, and her hips looked almost boyish, they were so narrow. And she was supposed to be for *him*? The grownest thing about her were her high heels. There were times when Hustle was really wak, like he had totally lost the plot.

" 'Sup," responded Nate, looking past her.

An older girl with blond braids like skinny ropes down to her waist had her arms draped around Hustle's neck.

"Schoolie, Ky . . . Ky, Schoolie. And her friend Miss Bootylicious here is called . . . What's your name again?"

"Felice Kenyatta."

"*Riiight* . . . Felice Kenyatta."

"But I go by Fly."

Hustle licked his fleshy lips. "*Yeeaaah.* Fly and Ky. I'm *feelin'* that. So, uh, Schoolie, these ladies say they hungry. What you think 'bout us going up to Harlem Pizza on 137th? The tab's on me, of course, since the CD me and P. Diddy hooked up drops next week."

If eyes could bore holes through flesh, Hustle would've been on his way to the nearest emergency room. What CD? Then Nate flashed on a perfect revenge.

"With the mad cash you got up front for your own CD, plus what they paid you for the dope rhymes you penned for Missy—"

"Missy *Elliott?*" squealed Ky.

". . . and the Neptunes . . ."

"*Ooooo*, I *love* me some Neptunes . . ." oozed Fly.

". . . you should take these sweet girls someplace nice like Sylvia's or Spoonbread. Ain't that right, girls?"

"Miss Maude's Spoonbread Too s'pose to be *off the hook*," said Fly, her eyes big.

"Mama took me there last year when I turned thirteen!" exclaimed Ky, forgetting she'd told Hustle she was "sixteen going on seventeen." "Hmmm, I loves me some beef short ribs," she said, swallowing. "Y'all hafta try the pie alley mode!"

Hustle looked from Nate, to Ky, to Fly, and back to Nate, who was smiling and nodding in agreement with everything the girls said. The table was going to be nice and hefty.

"Ah-ight, that's cool, Schoolboy. You da pimp."

The two couples set out for Harlem's most popular Southern-style restaurant. Fly and Ky were almost skipping, arm-in-arm, giggling and whispering to each other. Behind them, Hustle and Nate marched in silence, the one glowering, the other beaming. Forty-seven dollars later, the girls said, "Thank y'all," and waved goodbye. They had to be getting home.

Their "dates" gone, the boys couldn't help but laugh.

"Why you do me like that, Schoolie, that was *wrong*. Them hoochies put the *o* in *hooong*ry. You saw how much they *ate*?!"

"That's what you get for *hustlin'* little girls. Why you mix *me* up in it? I'm minding my neck in the library, not bothering nobody . . ."

"I had to do *something*. You was in there forever. I was bored. It's all good though. Least they was nice to look at. I mean, when they cheeks wasn't stuffed with food."

Night had blown in on a cool wind. Nate adjusted his cap and flipped the collar up on Eli's jacket. Hustle pulled on his hood. He liked that it kept his head warm. But he especially liked that it also intimidated people. They were passing by the red art deco doors of the Lenox Lounge when Nate's cell phone vibrated against his chest.

"Yeah?" he answered. After a brief conversation he snapped the phone shut. "It's been real, but I got a better deal!"

"Oh, so you gon' kick ya boy to the curb just like that. Gotta be a hoochie. *Gots* to be."

Nate snatched Hustle playfully by the arm and spun him around. "Shantay ain't a hoochie, sucka! She's my girl."

Shantay Reed, a sixteen-year-old high schooler, was one of four fatherless Reeds, all only half brothers and sisters. An average student, she had her eye on the usual professional mirages that mesmerize girls her age. An article in a magazine about teen fashion got her to dreaming about becoming a model. After being the ninety-ninth caller to Hot 99 FM and winning a ticket to see Missy and Timbaland at the Apollo, she wanted to rap. She saw a TV documentary about boxing champion Lucia Rijker and . . . In short, Shantay was an impressionable teenager without much real direction to her life.

The summer day when Shantay and Nate first stole glances at each other on Adam Clayton Powell Boulevard, they were both fifteen. He was cute and didn't stare at her chest the way nasty boys did. She was pretty and carried a notebook she said was her diary (begun after watching an Anne Frank after-school movie special). They liked each other and began hanging out together when he was home for holidays. They made no promises, swore no forevers . . . but they liked each other.

"Did *I* do that?" Nate brought his face closer.

Shantay's hand flew to her neck. "What?"

"That," he said, holding in his hand a long black extension that had come loose from Shantay's hair.

"You be wildin', that's how they break off." She giggled and scooted up against him, hiding her face in his neck. "I hafta buy more anyhow."

A gust rattled through the wedge-shaped hole in the top corner of the window. They pulled the flowered comforter close around their naked shoulders and snuggled in each other's arms. He loved the musky smell of her skin and marveled at its softness. Most of the time he abandoned himself to their teenage pleasures, but occasionally he still felt self-conscious.

"Your moms ever say anything about, you know, me staying over?"

Shantay sucked her teeth. "She don't care! Her man be up in here. My sisters' scrubs be up in here. My *brother* even be sneakin' mens in his room."

"Whuuuut?!"

"Hey, that's his thing. Ain't hurtin' nobody. I'm like, wha-evuh."

Through the broken window resounded the mighty choir of the First Corinthian Baptist Church just next door.

Nate kissed her forehead. The sound of gospel prompted a question.

"You believe in God?"

"Of course," she declared. "Everybody do. Don't you?"

"Yeah, why not? So why ain't you in church on a Sunday morning?"

" 'Cause I'm here wichoo. Why *you* ain't in church?"

" 'Cause the choir at Greater Central Baptist near where *I* live don't sound *half* this good. So I come over to listen to yours. Come here, girl." He pulled her closer.

They lingered together most of the morning, then jumped out of bed, famished. After devouring whatever they could find in the refrigerator and cabinets, Shantay said she had to meet her girl Booquana at the hair place. Nate reminded her he was going back to school that evening. There was nothing she could do. Booquana would be out there waiting. They'd buy some hair, then go to Boo's place to do each other's extensions. Nate was disappointed but decided he'd give Randall a call since his afternoon was suddenly free.

Mrs. Whitely was relaxing on the sofa flipping through *Oprah Magazine*. Next to her sat Mr. Whitely, his feet propped up on the wood crate that served as an ottoman. He allowed himself one day off every week and enjoyed spending it watching sports. At the moment, his eyes were glued to the basketball game on television. The star teams of the WNBA, the New York Liberty and the Los Angeles Sparks, were battling at Madison Square Garden.

"Yesss!" cheered Mr. Whitely, leaping to his feet with both fists in the air. "Did you see *that*, baby?! Lisa Leslie went up for a dunk!"

Mrs. Whitely raised her eyes slowly from her page, a hint of a smirk on her mouth. "Thought you were rooting for New York, traitor."

"I *am*," he explained, sitting down again, "but when a foxy, six-foot sister goes sailing through the air . . ."

"Foxy? You never mention *Shaq's* looks. Why don't you just quit while you're ahead, Jared, before I get *real* mad."

He took her in his arms, laughing, and kissed her lips.

Eli surprised them. "All right, y'all! Get *jiggy* widdit!

As the song go, 'ain't nuthin' wrong . . . with a little bump and . . .' "

"Eli!" Mrs. Whitely wasn't a prude, but that kind of talk embarrassed her.

Mr. Whitely laughed hard.

"Y'all have a *real* nice Sunday afternoon," said Eli. "I'ma go shoot some hoops at the park. Come to think of it, I should apply for a coaching gig with them fly girls Pops is into. Show 'em a *real* baller's flava. Heh, heh." He put on a thick, mustard leather bomber.

"That's a pretty jacket. It's new?" asked Mrs. Whitely, ignoring her son's last comment.

"Sean Jean in the house. Courtesy of Mr. Hustle."

She shook her head. "I can't tell you what to do, and I know he's going to sell them anyway, but it's not right, having that boy out there stealing . . ."

"I don't tell him to steal. I just buy it when it's already stole. Anyway, he said he's planning on retiring from . . . um . . . recycling, once his rap thing blow."

Mr. Whitely said Eric was just another ghetto dreamer. "Why all you young folk think playing street ball and rhyming materialistic nonsense is going to make you rich? If I had a buck for every dropout, cop-out, and rubbed-out who was gonna *blow up* and *live large*, I'd* be the one rich. What you guys need to do is learn a trade or a skill, something you can use your whole adult life, and put it to work for you."

Eli tilted his black leather cap to the side. "Like tightening hubcaps?"

Mr. Whitely sat upright. "Exactly like tightening hubcaps. It's keeping food in *your* mouth."

In the silence that followed, father, mother, and son simply watched each other to see who'd make the next move, and whether it would be offensive or defensive. Eli did.

"You right, Pops, you right. I wish I brought in more cash from the odd jobs I do around the neighborhood . . . I'ma see if old Burghardt will up my hours."

His father softened as well. "I'll talk to him tomorrow. Watch your back out there. You going to Convent Park?"

"St. Nick. They know me down there, so I get picked up faster." A thought caught his attention. "I see Nate and Hustle hung out all night, those hoods."

"No they didn't," said Mrs. Whitely. "Nate called from Shantay's around—what time was it, eleven, eleven-thirty?—saying he was spending the night over there. He should be walking in the door any minute now."

Eli made a sound like "hmmph," then said, "I'm outta here. Bye."

"Bye, Eli."

"Bye, son."

He snatched the door shut with all his might.

The atmosphere in Shantay's room had been heavy and close, and now Nate hungrily inhaled the crisp air blowing in off the Hudson River. He cut across 125th Street to Martin Luther King Jr. Boulevard and strolled up St. Nicholas Avenue past the park, where he stood for a while watching a basketball game. No one he knew was playing. He continued up to 145th, checking the address he'd written on a piece of chewing gum wrapper.

The town house where Randall lived was directly in front of him. He rang the doorbell and was caught off guard by the sound of chimes. Randall opened the door with a flourish. Dressed in Levi's with holes in the knees and a Columbia varsity sweatshirt missing half the felt on its lettering, the founding partner of the Stone and Lee architecture firm looked just as he did when the two had first met.

"Behold the wunderkind! Enter!"

He inspected his guest from head to toe.

"Excuse me. I mistook you for someone else, a Fletcher scholar I know. But you're that homey from BET's *Rap Attack*, right?"

"Ha, ha, Randall. Why you gotta dis?"

"*Why you gotta dis.* What is this *dialect?* Is Fletcher offering Ebonics classes now? Get in here and sit down so I can teach you English."

The entryway glinted with stained glass, mirrors, and miniature chandeliers. Randall read the tag of Nate's jacket as he hung it up in a nook to the side of the double doors.

"What's with the ghetto fabulous look?" He raised his heavy eyebrows and rubbed his trim mustache. "This way, Nate, I want you to meet someone."

The boy Nate was when "Mr. Stone" interviewed him for SOAR had been awestruck by the cocky math major with the Schwarzenegger physique and Einstein brain. Nate the adolescent was still in awe as he followed his former adviser through finely detailed rooms with lofty ceilings, mahogany and oak panel interiors, ornate carved mantelpieces, and even more stained glass. Nate felt impressed and awkward, and a touch envious. *This* was how he was going to hook things up for his folks once he had mad money like Randall.

"Man, Randall, you're living *large.*"

Randall nodded. What else *could* he do? He knew he was living very well, not just by Harlem standards but by *any* standards.

"And largely living . . . that is, on the rare occasions

when I'm not working. You rang up at the perfect time."

They arrived at a room off of what the host proudly called "the master bedroom." He tapped his knuckle on the door.

"Our guest is here. Mr. Nathaniel Whitely."

Nate took a step back.

A young man of slight build with very black hair, hooded eyes, and a broad smile appeared. His Ralph Lauren polo shirt was frayed at the collar and his Old Navy jeans faded.

"Hi, Nathaniel, I've heard tons about you. I'm Kenny, Randy's partner . . ."

Nate grunted like a boxer taking a blow.

". . . at the firm. Draftsman. Can I get you something to drink? A snack?"

"No, thanks. I'm good."

The men sat on a leather sofa the color of dark chocolate. Nate sat on a chair with curved armrests and feet, upholstered in a silky brown-striped fabric.

"So . . ." said Randall, beaming.

"So . . ." responded Nate, squirming.

Kenny asked Nate about Fletcher, what classes he was taking, how the teachers were, what the other students were like. Once Nate got into talking about the huge campus, the paper he was working on for multicultural studies, the Falcons' lacrosse league record, crazy Spencer Adams, and a nice-looking girl he had his eye on, he relaxed and even began to enjoy himself. The conversation turned to music. Nate admitted to being "blown away" that Kenny liked hip-hop and was into MC Jin.

"Of course! You know I'ma kick it with the first Chinese rap star: 'If you make one joke about rice or karate / NYPD will be in Chinatown lookin' for your body.' Now *that's* a lyric."

Randall, strictly an R&B man, clasped his hands together and said, "Lord deliver us!" In the tone of a victor, he recounted how he had cornered Nate's parents in their apartment and literally demanded they let Nate go to Fletcher.

"But I thought they were into it all along."

"No they were *not*, Nate. They worried it might be too much of a . . . cultural change for you. Remember, you were just a baby then."

He confessed, to Nate's surprise, how difficult it had been for *him* to get used to that "bourgeois, private school world"—and *he* was "born to be bougie."

Kenny crowed. "That's funny! 'Randy Stone—born to be bougie.' I *love* it!" He couldn't stop laughing. "On that note . . ." He stood and left the salon.

Nate smiled, fidgeted, rubbed his chin, and smiled a

second time. "Mr. Stone," he began urgently, "I mean Randy . . . Randall. I didn't know you were . . . gay. Not that I have a problem with it." He didn't really know whether he had a problem with it or not.

Randall stared at him, with a serious look on his face.

Confusion and embarrassment filled Nate's face. "I'm *not* gay," Randall said, sounding almost indignant. "*Kenny* is." With that, he exploded with laughter.

Kenny returned carrying a tray crowded with juices, sodas, bottled water, pistachio nuts, olives stuffed with feta, Dorito chips, and a bowl of some kind of dip Nate peered at.

"Hummus," said Kenny. "Try it, it's delicious. So what's so funny?"

Randall caught his breath. "Mr. Whitely here said—"

"Nothing, man! I was just telling Randall this joke I heard at school about . . ."

Nate caught Randall's eyes and held them pleadingly, just for a second.

"You wouldn't get it anyway, Kenny," said Randall. "It's ethnic."

Kenny made a face. "*I'm* ethnic too, brother. And *I'm* the one who tells *you* all the jokes."

There was more conversation, a tour of both floors of the house, a look through Kenny's album, CD, and DVD music collection, and more chips and hummus, which Nate liked. It was time for him to leave. He had to get home, spend time with his folks, and pack up his stuff before hopping the train back. Randall told him to call, write, e-mail, or just show up whenever he wanted. The trio shook hands and parted ways.

Back home, Nate was chided by his parents for leaving them the leftover crumbs of his time. He cracked them up with his tale about making Hustle take him and the two girls to Spoonbread Too. Mrs. Whitely said she had been meaning to drop by the restaurant and pay a visit to her buddy Norma, the owner. Mr. Whitely bemoaned not having a "cooking wife." Nate dazzled them with details of Randall's house. Mr. Whitely said all that would be a bit much for him, personally. Mrs. Whitely asked if Randall had a guest room for her. Nate didn't mention Kenny and Randall turning out gay and all. He was still trying to get his brain around it. Shantay was probably right. Big deal.

Later that evening, Nate packed up his knapsack, embraced his parents, and headed for the subway to Grand Central, where he'd change clothes and board the train to Edessa Hills. He had wanted to say goodbye to Eli and tell him to chill out on the drug dealing, but Eli wasn't around. At the subway steps he tried to reach Shantay on her cell phone. He left a message.

Nate and Spencer walked across the leaf-covered campus on their way to lacrosse practice. They had an upcoming game against Drucker Preparatory School, whose team, the Druids, had clobbered the Falcons last month on Drucker's campus. This would be the final match between the rival teams. Talk of cannibalism was in the air.

"This is how we're gonna crush Sucker Prep," said Spencer, jabbing his crosse like a spear. He wore the crimson jersey and shorts of the Fletcher Falcons. Cleated shoes hung from one shoulder and an oversized bag from the other. "Those thugs are chopped liver."

"Ground meat," said Nate, massive in his arm guards and shoulder pads. "Big Macs to go." The Falcons' best midfield player, Nate was known for his speed, endurance, and agility, and nicknamed "Body" for his powerful body checks.

A girl in army boots approached. The collar of her school blazer was turned up and the shredded hem of her flag-adorned dress dragged on the ground. Her hair was a red tangled mass of something resembling dreadlocks.

"Hi, Spence. Hi, Nathaniel. Uh, Spence, can I talk to you a sec?"

"At your service, fair Valerie."

They walked a few steps away. Nate waited. Spencer returned, tucking bills in his pocket.

"What'd she want?" asked Nate, although he knew.

"An ancient herbal remedy."

Spencer was one of the school's major pot dealers. Not a smoker but a businessman, he claimed. And not in it for money either, but to develop his business skills. He compared himself to "fellow outlaw entrepreneur" Joseph Kennedy, Sr., whose family fortune could be traced back to illegal booze sales. The administration was aware of the boy's activities but turned a blind eye. Its other eye was on the hefty annual donations the school received from Adams Global Electronics.

"I know you've got it all under control, Spence, but you should be more careful. It's not like people aren't hip to what you're doing. I've seen too many guys end up behind bars who thought they had everything under control."

Spencer stopped. "You're talking apples and bananas. That's like comparing cocaine importers and crack dealers. Who's going down? Not the guy with money, connections, and lawyers, that's for sure."

Eli popped into Nate's head. He wanted to sit his brother down and give him the same talk, but it seemed harder to do with family than with a friend.

"Remember last year when the police came on campus to bust all the dealers?" continued Spencer. "They had to let the headmaster know in advance, and as a courtesy, so he said, he let *us* know in advance. The school didn't want the bad headline 'Preppie Pot Pushers Busted at the Fletcher School.' That kind of publicity hurts fundraising."

"How wrong is *that*, Spence, when lots of people are locked up right now for the same thing?"

"I'm not saying it's right, I'm just saying it *is*. Now, stop fretting over me like a Jewish mother and let's go prepare for *war*."

They reached Kennedy Field and joined their teammates, already divided up into attackers, midfielders, defenders, and goalkeepers. At the far end of the field the girls' team, the Furies, split into six defensive and six offensive players, were practicing with intensity. The boys ran through a series of plays they'd been working on over the past couple of weeks.

Coach Guy Thomas, a former college football star and competitive equestrian who doubled as the school's riding instructor, blew hard on his whistle. The boys collapsed to the ground in a chaos of crosses, gloves, helmets, and yellow, white, and orange balls. The coach paced past, walked around, and stepped over his players. There was something of the highway patrolman in his impenetrable sunglasses and bulky thighs.

"We're not *golfing*. You're supposed to *run* with the sticks, not stand there! Lacrosse is a game of attack and defense! Why d'ya think the Indians called it 'the little brother of war,' 'cause they were *poets*? This is *combat*, men, not badminton. The Furies' attackers over there got more guts than *you* guys. The objective, soldiers, is to use your sticks to send the ball through the goalposts of the enemy. Whitely, keep a foot on the ground when you check a runner, the refs are generous with fouls. Adams, you got hands, you got a body: *use* them—don't just defend with the stick. And Hamilton, what's with all the long throws? You're not on *Star Search*. Try passing the ball. Now, everybody listen up. I'm gonna go over formation and deployment one more time."

Armond Hamilton was a sophomore whose ego radiated around him like a helium-filled aura. Armond's father was a prominent black lawyer who, thanks to a celebrity clientele with a tendency to murder their spouses, speed from hit-and-run accidents, shoot their way out of posh discos, and sexually abuse fans, had become a wealthy celebrity himself. The son's habit of introducing himself by name, pausing, then adding, "of the Washington, D.C., Hamiltons," had won him few friends. Nate was one of the few. For him, Armond had at least one redeeming quality—he was black, and there weren't that many of them around.

Armond flopped down, panting and sweating, next to Nate.

"Coach must be on meth today. He's trying to kill us."

Nate laughed. "I *know*. It's an ego thing because Drucker kicked our butts last time."

"And probably will this time too," said Armond. "They're animals."

"But we got heart." Nate hated losing and gave the games his all.

"Hey, I'm as competitive as the next dude, but heart's not gonna get you real far when a buffalo's coming at you. Hearts are for Valentine's Day." He squinted into the distance. "And what I wouldn't give for *hers*."

Nate followed Armond's eyes. They were focused in the direction of the girls' team and fixed on an offensive player racing across the field with the grace and strength of a fine stallion pampered to perfection. Mastering her stick as if it were an extension of her arm, she caught a high throw on the run, deftly swerved and leapt past defenders, and made a perfect blind pass backward over her shoulder to a well-positioned teammate.

This wasn't the first time Nate had watched Willa Ellsworth Matthews. The truth was, despite having a girlfriend already, he was harboring a major crush on Willa. Her side scored and the girls all cheered and whooped. Willa was standing with her hands on her knees catching her breath, when abruptly she looked, or so it seemed to Nate, directly at him, as though she felt his gaze.

Despite the distance separating them, it was indeed possible. The sensation of being explored by admiring eyes was as familiar to Willa as slipping into a favorite warm coat. She was, after all, perfectly proportioned, solidly athletic, and had smooth, flawless skin the color of rich caramel. Her most striking feature, though, was her eyes. They were pale and held no fixed color but rather took on certain hues of her clothing. The pale blue of the blouse she wore to assembly. The stormy gray of the sweatshirt she jogged in. The dark brown of the baseball cap atop a head full of nappy curls.

"What you wouldn't give for whose *what?*" responded Nate. "You're not even making sense." Sure, he panted and pined with the guys over cute Cathy Gleason or sexy Lizzy van Bruner, but having a thing for a girl like Willa . . . *that*, you kept secret.

"You're a dense dude. I *said* I'd give anything for her . . . um . . . heart. Just look at her, she's *so* hot. Too bad she's a stuck-up virgin snob."

"Natasha Scotia?"

"Are you *blind*, Nathaniel?! Willa!" He leaned forward. "God, look at that stretch."

The girls' team was warming down with jumping jacks, side bends, and stretches.

Nate untied and retied his cleats. "Oh, her. She's all right. My girl's better."

"All right? Willa Matthews is *all right?* Your girlfriend must be Halle Berry, Angela Bassett, and Vanessa Williams rolled into one if she's hotter than Willa! Willa sizzles."

Nate frowned. Armond was becoming irritating.

"Then ask her out, if you like her that much."

"I did. She looked right through me with those weird X-ray eyes and said"—he raised his voice an octave— " 'I don't date sophomores.' Maybe *you* should go for it, Nathaniel, seeing that you're both juniors."

Nate was through listening. "Don't be a jerk. I *told* you, I got a girl."

The coach blew the whistle again and the Fletcher Falcons spent the remainder of the afternoon on the battlefield, where they fought with crosses for possession of one of the small yellow balls.

Longer, colder evenings settled in, keeping the students in their dorms. On Nate's floor the usual music wars raged, rock blaring at one end of the hallway and rap pumping at the other. Nate had on sweats and sat cross-legged on a bed strewn with sandwich wrappers, crumpled snack bags, and pages of handwritten notes. One of the few students not to have a laptop, Nate had spent days doing research on school computers and in shelved books. He leaned against a dark, frayed chair pillow, a Christmas gift from his mother, closed his eyes, and pushed his earplugs in deeper. The paper he was presenting the next morning was done.

He yawned, rubbed his eyes, and checked his watch. It wasn't too late, not yet eleven-thirty. He reached for the telephone, then remembered he'd canceled his long-distance service to save money. He got his cell phone out of his jacket pocket. No, it was stupid to call Shantay without news, just wanting to hear her voice. They'd agreed to call each other only if it was on a phone card with real cheap rates, and he didn't have one. He set the radio clock for eight o'clock and fell asleep.

Multiculturalism Today was an elective open to anyone in the upper school. It attracted very distinct groups. Earnest white freshmen who sat in petrified silence, not sure whether it was politically correct to say handicapped or other-abled, black or African American, fat or full-bodied, gay or queer, Indian or Native American. Minority students proud to find themselves and their world the focus of at least one course. And blasé seniors of all types and stripes who filled the back rows, whispering and giggling, hoping to boost their GPA with what they considered an easy course. Most students, however, were genuinely inspired with curiosity about other people, other cultures, other religions.

Dr. Pat McKruma, a plump black self-described intellectual, had grown up in Oregon in a tidy middle-class neighborhood outside Portland. The race riots and urban violence of the sixties never reached the placid streets of her little town, but, transfixed in front of the family television, she had, in her own remote way, lived through them. And she wanted to *do* something, get *involved*, help. After graduating Yale, where she won honors in sociology, she began her career teaching in exclusive private schools. The Fletcher School had been her home for the past ten years, and although everyone else was on a first-name basis, Dr. McKruma, proud of being the only faculty member with an actual Ph.D., insisted she be called "Doctor." A request students did *not* find endearing.

"Come to order, class! Take your seats, please. Today we will hear from each of you a brief summary of the papers you have, or should have, handed in by now, papers which explore a unique manifestation of the multicultural integrative process in the American socio-economic contemporary landscape and highlight the political, the psychological, or the spiritual dimensionality of that process."

The class stared at her.

"Say *whuuuut?*" whispered Willa to her buddy Jeannette.

Jeannette Simpson had grown up in Brooklyn's Sheepshead Bay projects with her grandmother, Nanna, for whom the worst wrong was being "stuck-up." A crime for which Jeannette had convicted Pat McKruma at first sight.

"I have *no* idea," smirked Jeannette. "McKruma and Narcissus, twins separated at birth. She should buy a kitten and name it Life. Then she'd have one."

Willa barely choked back her laughter.

"Jeannette," asked the teacher, "a comment to share with the class?" Dr. McKruma couldn't fathom why a girl as bright as Jeannette seemed bent on irritating her, knowing it would hurt her grade. She secretly questioned the wisdom of admission policies that didn't provide for personality screening of these bright but angry underclass kids.

"No, Miss . . . I mean *Doctor* . . . McKruma."

"I thought not." She reviewed the class list. "Spencer Adams."

Spencer described his paper as a comparative look at the glorious past of white Anglo-Saxon Protestants in America—from the brave settlers who founded the country to the robber barons who industrialized and enriched it—and the tragic present of their descendants, left with a legacy of shame, no ethnic identity, and routinely bad press. A couple of students complained that a paper on WASPs was out of place in that class, but Dr. McKruma said multiculturalism had to embrace all groups, "including plundering Pilgrims."

In another paper, the plight of the vanishing farmer was described by a sleek, well-dressed girl with a pair of expensive sunglasses propped on her head. Her family of farmers held a majority interest in an agro-industrial conglomerate, and things were "just really, really hard" for her dad and grandpa, what with paying so much in taxes and not getting enough government support or anything. Someone's loud, fake sob made a number of kids laugh.

A boy wearing a No Brands T-shirt said his paper raged against the machinery of globalism, which was setting up a conformist world order where everybody ate hamburgers, wore Tommy Hilfiger, and auditioned for survival shows so they could swallow slugs and win a million bucks. Jeannette interjected that Tommy-wear was so played out it was like it was never in. Dr. McKruma warned Jeannette about interrupting the presentations and asked the student impatiently what, if anything, his paper had to do with ethnic cultures integrating mainstream American culture. His answer, that rebels against the spiritual wasteland were scorned and discriminated against, aggravated the teacher even more.

"Has *anyone* done a paper based on a more, shall we say, traditional definition of the term *multiculturalism?*"

Nate raised his hand. He'd noticed what he thought was a church that seemed out of place in Harlem, so he researched it, and was surprised to find out it was a place of worship for black Jews. The back row giggled; other kids elbowed each other. Nate smiled. At first, he said, he couldn't believe it either, but his research uncovered pictures by a photographer named Alexander Alland of a black congregation, black rabbis holding the Torah, black cantors doing traditional Jewish rituals. It was like discovering relatives you didn't know you had. He explained that Ethiopians have followed the Jewish religion for centuries. And that New York

City has ten thousand black Jews whose lodge, called the Royal Order of Ethiopian Hebrews, is right on his street.

Armond said he would have to see the photos with his own eyes. Willa thanked Nate for raising awareness. A soft-spoken blonde said she thought "the Jews and the blacks, uh, Afro . . . umm, *African*-Americans . . . didn't get along so great." Dr. McKruma explained that during the civil rights movement Jewish and African-American activists were on the front lines, where together they fought and sometimes died.

"The same people who hate blacks hate Jews, and vice versa," she said.

Spencer said, "Cool, sort of like that 'my enemy's enemy is my friend' thing."

"Something like that," said Nate. "Anyway, I really got into the whole subject and discovered that in the sixties, before everybody was into their own separate thing, blacks and Jews worked together. For example, in Mississippi three men were murdered by the Ku Klux Klan for helping register black people to vote."

"I know about that," interrupted a girl excitedly. "It was in the movies. One was black and two were white, right?"

"Yes," responded Nate. "A black Mississippi native and two Jews from New York. Everybody was outraged by the killings, which made national headlines only a month after President Johnson signed the Civil Rights Act of 1964. That same year"—he looked at an index card—"Martin Luther King, Jr., got the Nobel Peace Prize."

A boy listening sullenly in the front row raised his hand. "1964?! That was ages ago. What about the riots in Crown Heights, when all the black people attacked Jews because of a car accident. An *accident*. I'm sorry if this is politically incorrect or whatever, but what they did wasn't right."

"Oh, like running down a little boy because he's black *is?*" retorted the girl next to him.

"What are you talking about? Nobody ran down anyone! The driver, who just happened to be Jewish, lost control of his car."

"Okay, okay," said Dr. McKruma, raising both hands. "Dispassionate discourse, please. For those of you who may not be familiar with the event in question, several years ago in the Crown Heights section of Brooklyn, fighting broke out between blacks and Jews following a traffic *accident*"—she paused—"in which a seven-year-old black boy was killed. Existing tensions erupted and a Jewish man was stabbed to death. Nate, please go on."

"Well, what I try to show in my paper is that nowadays people only remember the bad things that happen, like in Crown Heights, but there used to be unity because of the bigotry and discrimination against both groups. But people should also remember that *other* groups like the Klan and the Aryan Nations still have the same unity *they* had *ages ago*"—he looked at the boy in the front row—"when two Jews and a brother were killed together." He thought saying "a brother" added a nice touch at the end.

"Well done, Nate. I look forward to reading it." The teacher looked around the room. "Who else?"

Several other papers were hurriedly presented by hungry students eager to get to lunch. At the end of class, the teacher thanked the speakers and reminded everyone that class participation counted for a big part of their overall grade. Willa and Jeannette ran into Nate in the hall.

"Good paper, Nathaniel," said Jeannette. "Big up Harlem."

"Thanks. Big up Brooklyn."

"Yes, very interesting," agreed Willa. "And I thought you were just a jock."

Until that moment, Willa Matthews had never spoken to him directly. She either avoided his eyes or looked straight through him. Always without a word. So that now the simple fact of her mouth—that full, pouty, lipsticked mouth—having held the words that floated his way like perfumed rose petals, caused his head to spin.

"Yeah . . . um . . . thanks."

The dining hall echoed with clinking cutlery and the drone of teenage chatter. Nate had joined Armond and a group of boys at a "girl-watching" table near a window. Still reeling from his Willa encounter, he devoured a mixed salad, glazed ham, a mound of cooked carrots, a large helping of rice, a side dish of kale, two rolls, a brownie, and lots of lemonade. The others cracked tapeworm jokes that would have sickened someone with a weaker stomach, but Nate laughed along with them, his mind lingering in the past. *And I thought you were just a jock . . . just a jock . . .* She had thought about him! Willa Matthews had for a sweet moment held him in her mind, and thought he was just a jock.

The beaming sun intensified the blue of the sky and the green grass field. The bleachers shook from the rhythmic stomping of feet. Red banners fluttered in the wind like flocks of redbirds. Leggy cheerleaders shaking pom-poms of crimson and white kicked, leapt, and bounced. Fletcher boys and girls chanted in one voice: "*Fal*cons! *Fal*cons! *Fal*cons!" A group of Drucker Prep supporters in black jerseys who'd made the trip with the team shouted, "Gimme a D! Gimme an R! Gimme a U-C-K!" but before they could ask, "What's that spell?!" their voices were drowned out by the repeated roar of "Druck Sucks!"

The judge, referee, and coaches gathered at the officials' table. Players assembled on the field and blasted through a series of jumping jacks, waist bends, and push-ups, the home team in crimson jerseys and shorts, the visitors in black. The exhilarated boys shoved, kicked, punched, and body-slammed one another as they psyched up for the rough physical contact that was not only permitted but required.

"Willa! Check out the body on that Druid," whispered Jeannette, pointing to a massive player slashing the air with a short crosse. "I'd hate to get in *his* path."

"Oh you would? Now *that's* something new."

Laughing, Jeannette gave Willa a poke in the ribs. They attended all the home games, Jeannette to cruise boys and Willa to see new plays and learn strategy. And sneak looks at boys.

"Look at them, J," said Willa. "They are so violent. Our team relies on stick skills, but boys just want to whack the hell out of each other. That's because they're all on drugs—testosterone."

Jeannette agreed. And speaking of drugs, she didn't understand why Spencer Adams was even on the team when the school had strict anti-drug rules and everybody knew he was dealing. A total double standard was in effect. If it were Nathaniel or Armond, they'd be out the front gate in no time.

"The game's starting!" said Willa. "Let's move down."

The girls scrambled to the middle section of the bleachers and slid in next to their schoolmates.

"Gear up!" commanded Coach Thomas. "And take no prisoners!" The Falcons got into their protective shoulder pads, face-guard helmets, and thick padded gloves. Freshman Luke Cameron, the quickest attacker, checked the crosses of his two attack players to make sure they were the shorter, regulation forty-inch ones. Nate and the other two midfielders wore arm and rib pads along with the standard fare because of the brutal resistance "middies" could meet moving the ball across the field. As goalkeeper, Spencer was directly in the line of fire from high-speed shots traveling up to seventy miles per hour. He wore special leg and shin guards, a chest pad, and a throat protector.

Nate checked his face mask and chin pad, clutched his crosse, and raced to the center of the field for the opening face-off. He planted himself opposite a thick Druid and fixed his eyes on the white ball the referee placed between the sticks of the opponents. A whistle shrilled. Nate's body jolted. The players struggled to control the ball. Nate dueled with the skill of a fencer, the metal shaft of his crosse striking and knocking his opponent's. Voices cried out.

"Come on, Nathaniel! Fight!"

"Shove him!"

He slammed his upper body against the other player. The boy stumbled backward. Nate scooped up the ball in the pocket of his stick and flew down the field. The bleachers boomed.

"*Fal*cons! *Fal*cons! *Fal*cons!"

A dull drone was all he heard as he sprinted and dodged in cleats towards the Druids' goalpost. Rhythmic bursts of breath and the pounding of his heart filled his head. He relished the burn in his thighs and the strain in his shoulders. The Falcon attackers were downfield, their eyes on Nate. Luke was closest to the goal. Nate raised his crosse to make the pass. A hard whack on his glove nearly knocked the stick from his hands. In an instant, two husky Druid defenders were poking, slapping, and hitting Nate's stick and gloved hands to dislodge the ball.

The Druid fans went wild.

"*Deeeee*-fense! *Deeeee*-fense!"

The ball popped out of the net of Nate's crosse and went rolling. Groans and cheers mingled and filled the air. As Luke turned to lunge for the ball, which had rolled within a few feet of him, he was shoved from behind. The force of the impact sent him sprawling facedown. The referee blew his whistle.

"Foul! Foul! That's a foul!" Coach Thomas was jumping up and down.

"Illegal body check," the referee declared. "Pushing. One minute."

Under a rainfall of jeers and a sprinkling of cheers, the Druid player ran to the box to wait out his penalty.

"What cheaters," complained Jeannette.

"Cheaters!" cried a girl behind her, as if she'd been looking for that exact word.

A boy sitting nearby swore he knew for a fact that half of Drucker Prep was on meth and that's why the Druids were so wild.

Willa said, "Poor Nate. I know how that feels, to be so close and then, bam!"

When play resumed, a Druid defender kicked a loose ball to a teammate who caught and passed it in one sweeping motion to a fast-moving midfielder. Determined to make the block, Armond bore down on him waving his crosse. The defender threw the ball over his shoulder to a powerful attacker who hurled it at the Falcons' goal. Spencer dove at the ball and took the shot straight to his chest.

As the first quarter stretched into the second, Nate and the midfielders raced the length of the field, catching and passing to their teammates and clashing repeatedly with quick, aggressive Druids. The continuous movement and flow of the game filled the boys with sheer exuberance. Its violent contact glutted them with passion. Nate felt particularly provoked by the Druids, who deliberately pushed his crosse with their hands, swung at his helmet, and checked him even when he didn't have the ball. At the Falcon end of the field Druids charged and hurled the hard rubber ball past Armond and the other two defenders, who seemed to shrink from the raging attackers. Spencer threw his body left and right, absorbing shot after shot. But a few whipped by. At halftime, the Falcons were losing 3–0.

Coach Thomas rotated in two new midfielders to replace the ones complaining of fatigue. Nate insisted on staying in. He was the best middie, not just for his speed and stick skills but because of his hustle and stamina. Armond rotated out after taking a blow to the back of the neck.

"Take the short guy who hit Armond," shouted Spencer to Nate. "They'll pass to him!" The Druid attacker ran up the sidelines. The two Falcon defenders chased the player carrying the ball, who tossed it in a high arc to the attacker. The ball and Nate arrived at the same moment. Holding both ends of the crosse, the boy raised the shaft so Nate would collide with it. Nate tumbled to the ground. Willa jumped to her feet. Coach Thomas howled. Spencer yanked off his gloves and helmet and charged the boy. Furious fighting broke out on the field, and minor scuffles in the bleachers. Whistles blew nonstop as coaches and officials rushed to separate the warriors. The game was stopped.

Spencer's sanction was tough. He would not be allowed to play in the next two games against other schools. That evening, Nate and Spencer skipped dinner in the dining hall to eat pizza and watch DVDs in Spencer's room.

"So what got into you, Spencer? Don't get me wrong, I appreciate you backing me up, but I was all right. Now you're suspended."

Spencer shook his head. "I don't care. I know you can take a wallop, but it was the principle. Those Drucker Preppies are creeps, the way they were going after you."

"Hey, it's a rough game. Everybody takes a beating."

Spencer shook his head again. "They were on *your* case, Nathaniel."

Nate put down his slice and wiped his mouth. "What, it was personal?"

"Yep. In a general sense, it was personal."

Nate didn't follow.

"I have a couple of . . . business contacts . . . at Drucker. I hear things. The Druids are thugs who'd do anything, foul anyone, to win. But there are some jerks on the team who deliberately go after 'non-WASPs,' to use their term. Blacks, Catholics, Chinese, Jews, it doesn't matter to these jerks. If your blood's not Pilgrim blue, you're a target. Remember all the hits you took in that last game? Not as many as today, but, still, there were a lot."

"Yeah, I remember, but that's lacrosse. I didn't think they were . . ."

"They were."

"But they can't even see us through our face guards."

"Don't be naive, Nate. You've seen them without their gear on, right? Well, they've seen us plenty of times. Believe me, they know who's who."

Nate was stunned. Other than a bad vibe here or a slight attitude there, nothing racial had come up since he'd been at Fletcher. The place was pretty cool, even if most of the students were white kids from money. There were a few blacks, some Hispanics, a number of Asians, even three students from overseas. Drucker Prep was probably the same. He grew angry.

"Who was he anyway, what's his name? I couldn't really see what he looked like because of the face guard. I'm ready to hop the bus over to Sucker Prep right now. I've got something for him, and for *all* those punk Pilgrims who can't stand to see a black guy doing good."

Spencer took a gulp of ginger ale. "It's not just about 'black,' Nathaniel, it's everybody who's not like them— you, me, anybody."

Nathaniel smirked. "You? Hey, you're my mentor and a good guy and all, but you *are* them."

"No, I'm not," said Spencer, staring absently at the TV screen. The movie had been over for a while. "I'm not a WASP. My real name's Adamowicz. My great-grandfather changed it when he left Poland right before the war. We're Jewish."

Nate stared at him. "Wait, wait, wait . . . You're tripping me out here . . . What about your ancestors who founded the country and all that, the WASP Pilgrims?"

Spencer smiled. "We reinvented ourselves. That's what the family chose, so that's what I do."

They sat in silence. The TV screen flickered. Spencer pressed Eject and the DVD drawer slid open. Nate leaned back in the leather chair.

"So when you whipped that Druid's behind . . . that wasn't just for the team, that was for me?"

"For us both. The enemy of my enemy is my friend, right?"

Nathaniel smiled. "Right, my man." They shook hands on it.

The pace of school quickened with assignments, exams, and papers. Weekends were busy with Student Center offerings—movies, concerts, lectures by visiting alums. Nate called home from time to time to check in with everybody. They were fine, his mother would always say. At times he'd hear something else in her voice when he asked specifically about Eli. Worry. Fatigue. She'd just say, "Oh, you know that brother of yours," as if to shield Nate from negative distractions. But he knew from Hustle that Eli was messing up. He was reckless, stepping on the toes of some very unforgiving pushers and having too many close calls with the police. Nate would ask to talk to him, but Eli was never there. Sometimes Nate would manage to catch Shantay at home. But not very often.

A knock at the door startled him. He was munching pretzels and concentrating on French verbs. Between the irregular verbs and the verbs that were exceptions to *all* the rules, none of the conjugations were making sense. He hoped the visitor was Spencer, who'd been slacking off on the French tutoring because he was so busy himself.

"It's open!"

Willa Matthews stepped into the room. She had on a dark gray Gap turtleneck with her blazer and wore sandblasted jeans with gray suede Joan & David boots.

"Hi. Haven't seen you around."

Nate rose to his feet too quickly and banged his knee. "Owww," he moaned, rubbing it.

"Ouch," she said with a chuckle.

"Have a seat," he said, hopping over to a chair and throwing the clothes on it to the floor. "I've been busy with school stuff. Got a French test coming up." He could barely raise his eyes to meet the gray of Willa's. "Want some pretzels?"

She sat down. "No, that's okay. Why're you taking French? Everybody speaks Spanish."

Nate shrugged and sat on the bed. "I don't know. Do something different. Maybe I'll visit Haiti or Senegal." He didn't tell her the real reason he chose French. That his mother's dream was to one day visit Paris, and he fantasized that they'd go together. Didn't want to sound like a mama's boy.

Willa looked around the room. "Where's the rest of your stuff?"

"Right here. This is it." His neck felt tight. Most of the time it was easy for him to talk to girls, but this one . . . Maybe it was those weird eyes. He felt uncomfortable around her. He couldn't think of anything to say.

She yawned.

He cringed. "So, uh, you have any tests coming up?"

No, she said, but she had a paper due in English. "How are you feeling, by the way? Recovered? That last game against Drucker was the rowdiest I've ever seen. And that's not counting the fight at the end."

The blow had knocked the wind out of him, he said, that was all.

"And Spencer! That was something, the way he

pounced on the guy who whacked you. I'm against brawls, but it was kind of cool to see Spencer go there—he's usually so Mr. Unemotional WASP. I was surprised."

Nate remembered his conversation with Spencer. "Yeah, Spencer has *lots* of surprises up his sleeve."

There was more quiet.

"You never got hurt in a girls' game? How did you get into lacrosse in the first place? Do you have a brother into it? You have brothers and sisters?" Suddenly he had almost too much to say.

"Oh, just because it was different. Like you and French. I'd done tennis and soccer. And Fletcher's a major lacrosse school. I thought I'd give it a try and I turned out to be fairly good."

"Fairly good? It seems you're the best player on the team."

She laughed.

"Can I ask you a personal question, Willa?"

She grimaced. "Why? What?"

He twisted his neck from side to side. "What color are your eyes?"

She rolled them.

Nate flinched. He regretted asking.

She sighed and glanced towards the door. "Is that supposed to be some kind of come-on?"

"No! No, man. It's just that they seem to change a lot."

She observed him for a while, like she was debating something in her head. "I came by to invite you to Thanksgiving dinner at my parents' house. They said I could bring friends from school. Jeannette'll be there. And I'm asking Spencer, since you guys are friends."

Nate watched her mouth move. He fell into the gray sky of her eyes.

"Hellooo? Should I say it in French?"

He spent every Christmas at home, but had once spent Thanksgiving at school because he had so much schoolwork. It would probably be okay. He'd call his mother that evening and let her know his plans.

"Um . . . yeah, that'd be great. Definitely. I like meeting people's folks. Yeah."

"You won't like mine. They're both totally into the black Greek thing."

"You mean there're black Greeks too, like Ethiopian Jews? We have some of *everything* in us."

Laughing lit up her eyes and brought out her dimples. "Nooo, it's completely different. That's so funny! You don't know about the black Greek system? It's these secret societies with Greek names that you join in college. My whole family's into it—parents, uncles, aunts. Dad's an Alpha Phi Alpha."

Nate understood nothing of what she was saying but felt relieved to be off the topics of eye color and come-ons. He liked seeing her laugh.

"So what's the point?" he asked.

"Grips, chants, and steps."

"Grips, chants, and steps," he repeated. "Right."

"Secret handshakes, weird sounds, and dance routines. Once, my mom ran into one of her Alpha Kappa Alpha sorority sisters on the street and they started squealing. *Loud.* It was *very* embarrassing. Anyhow, the black Greeks claim they're into community service, but mostly they go around feeling superior and networking for jobs. It's very exclusive, elitist, and lame."

"So what gets you in? Big money?"

"Try big bruises. You have to let the members punch, slap, and kick you. They can also pound you with wooden paddles or anything else they choose. Some kids have actually died, can you believe it?! You finally make it to college and then get beaten to death with a rubber tire by some crazy frat rat. It's sick. I'll *never* pledge."

"Man, that's deep! You sure I should meet your folks?"

She stood. "It'll be fine. Dad's a heartless judge and Mom's a snobby insurance executive. But the food'll be good."

Images of fried chicken, macaroni and cheese, collard

greens, yams, sweet potato pie, and golden brown corn bread flooded his mind and watered his mouth. He excitedly noted the address and directions. After Willa left, Nate closed the door, locked it, and dropped to the floor. There he lay, breathing hard and smiling at the ceiling.

"Guess who's coming to dinner?"

"I dunno, Sidney Poitier? My mother has the video." Jeannette was too busy going through Willa's closet to make a serious guess. "*This* cute little combo might fit me." She pressed pants and a blazer of blue velvet corduroy against herself. "Can I wear it? I don't have anything nice and your folks are so . . . *bourgeoisie*."

Willa rose slowly from the vanity table, wearing fresh mascara, eyeliner, and La Perla boxer briefs and a sport bra. Her eyes, now light brown, were trained on the outfit Jeannette held up.

"Put . . . down . . . my . . . *very* . . . expensive . . . Elie Tahari. Or else."

Jeannette wobbled her head. "Well, *excuuuuse* me."

Willa reached in the closet and pulled out a denim jersey dress on a hanger. "Here. Betsey Johnson."

Jeannette frowned. "I don't care *whose* name's on it, it's still a smock made out of dungaree material. I want something fancy. *You're* gonna be all dolled up."

"I'm wearing plain ol' pants."

"Right. I know you and your 'plain ol' pants.' They're probably some two-hundred-dollar Elly Taj Mahali–whatever one of a kinds." She glimpsed a navy blue wool sweater on the bed. "What about *that?*"

At the rate they were getting dressed, the girls were going to be late for their ride. The school chef, part owner of a French restaurant in Inwood, was going to drop them off at Willa's house—if they were ready to go by two o'clock.

Willa shook her head. "Not! *I'm* planning to wear that." She looked at the wall clock. "It's twenty to two. Jacqueline's gonna be here any minute."

"You're the one running around in your drawers. All I really need is a top and I'm good to go."

"All right, take it. I'll wear the wool turtleneck with the cardigan. But don't get it all pitted out. That's an Eileen Fisher."

"Ooooo," sighed Jeannette, "an Eileen Fisher! Never heard of her. Why do you wear so many different brands anyway?"

"They're not brands, they're designers."

"Brands, designers, names, what have you. That's

wasted money. Me, I stick with one label—Sale." She pulled on the sweater and slid her arms over her chest and shoulders. "Mmmm, it's soft. I might have to keep it."

"Try it." Their eyes met defiantly. Then they burst out laughing.

Jeannette was curious. "So what important person *is* coming to dinner. Aside from me?"

Willa shrugged. "That's for me to know and for you to find out, my dear." She smiled and changed the subject to Jeannette's clothes. "I don't get it, J. Shouldn't you be sporting—oh excuse me, I mean rocking—Sean Jean and Phat Farm?"

Willa liked teasing her friend about growing up "in the hood" in Brooklyn. Other than Jeannette, she had no friends who weren't solidly middle class. There was Nathaniel, but she'd heard he lived in a luxurious Harlem brownstone, so she wasn't sure if he really counted. She was very curious about what she called homeboys and homegirls—their toughness, their *attitude*. And maybe a bit intimidated.

Jeannette didn't just take the bait, she swallowed it whole.

"Why you gotta go there?" she snapped, bumping Willa with her full-breasted chest. "Because I don't know all your Betty Boop, Sally Squarebutt designer chicks? Don't *make* me go project on you and kick ya Thanksgiving butt. If I'm gonna *front*, it won't be in overpriced, shapeless gym clothes covered with jumbo lettering. I ain't a billboard, I *gots* class."

Willa had cracked up in the middle of Jeanntte's outburst and was wiping tears from her eyes.

"*Ooooo*," she breathed, "I'm *afraaaid.*"

In an instant the girls were shrieking, their arms and legs flailing as they yanked, tugged, and wrestled. A knock sounded at the door. It was the chef, Jacqueline, right on time.

"Girls?" she called. "Ready? Girls?!"

Where was Spencer? He said he'd come by the room at four o'clock and it was already a quarter after. They had to be at the Matthewses' at five and it took an hour to get to Inwood. Nate ran a toothbrush across his eyebrows one last time. Then one last time he brushed down his short hair. Then wiped a cloth across his shoes. One last time. His hazel shirt was an OshKosh woven twill on loan from Spencer. A pair of simple black slacks completed his outfit. He put on a windbreaker over his blazer, patted his pockets for keys, wallet, Chap Stick, and breath mints, checked the directions to Inwood, and waited.

Spencer banged open the door, impeccable in tan

Dockers, an olive green button-down shirt, and a black lambswool sportcoat.

"You're late!"

"Relax! We're driving, remember? You want to drive part of the way?"

Like many young New Yorkers growing up with a 24/7 subway system, Nate had a permit but mostly just for ID. No, he didn't want to drive.

At the age of fourteen, Spencer saw from the window of his father's black Mercedes sedan the flash of a cherry red Karmann-Ghia ripping along the parkway. That one car became his sole desire, the *raison d'être* for getting his driver's permit. And that was the car in which he and Nate sped off en route to Thanksgiving dinner at the Inwood home of Judge and Mrs. Clarence Matthews.

Set between two rushing rivers, Inwood was a tranquil place, a Manhattan neighborhood with nothing of the feel of Manhattan. Lush forest, hiking trails, groomed gardens, and stunning views of the Palisades provided the green landscape for the area's cafés, art galleries, and cappuccino bars.

The Matthewses' triplex overlooked the cliffs and forest of a vast park. Judge Matthews was admiring the scene from his expansive terrace, one hand cradling the smooth bowl of a sleek Nording pipe and the other pressing blended flake tobacco into it with a stainless-steel tamper. His wife, stylish in a red cashmere crewneck sweater and wrap cardigan over black stretch velvet pants, glimpsed him on her way to the kitchen. He was contentedly smoking his pipe in his blue flannel pajamas and monogrammed Italian wool robe wrapped around his stout frame.

"Isn't it about time for you to get dressed, hon? The girls'll be here at three, and you still have to bring in wood for the fire and see what's making that knocking sound in the Jacuzzi."

A driven man obsessed with collecting corporate board memberships and speeding cases through his courtroom, the judge rarely allowed himself to enjoy a late morning. On the rare occasions when he did, he felt guilt from the pleasure such sloth gave him.

"I'll get to all of that, Lillian, in a minute."

And he did. By the time the girls pressed the buzzer, the fireplace was blazing, the Jacuzzi humming, and Judge Matthews was in a brown corduroy blazer, yellow silk dress shirt, and tan wool pleated trousers. He answered the door. Mrs. Matthews appeared, wiping her hands on a dishcloth.

"Hi, Dad. Hi, Mom. Happy Thanksgiving. *Ahhh*, yummy smells."

They gave each other affectionate pecks on the cheeks. Willa introduced Jeannette.

"Nice to meet you, Jeannette," Mrs. Matthews smiled.

"Welcome to our home, Jeannette," said the judge.

"You guys look nice," said Willa, giving her parents the once-over. At least they had *that* going for them.

"And so do you . . . both," responded Mrs. Matthews, her eyes lingering on Jeannette's very familiar-looking sweater. "Come in, sit down. Soda? Juice? Dinner will be a little while yet. The turkey's at least an hour away from our plates."

The girls took their overnight bags and headed upstairs to Willa's space, a full apartment with its own kitchen, bath, sitting room, and bedroom. Judge Matthews reviewed files and dictated decisions in his study. Mrs. Matthews set the table in the dining room, the skylights of its cathedral ceiling opening onto bouffant clouds.

Spencer drove up and down the blocks of Inwood in search of a parking space. The lots and garages were all full. The neighborhood teemed with nicely dressed people carrying bouquets, packages, and shopping bags. The expressway, busier than he'd expected, had worn a hole through his patience.

"Look at that beat-up Honda Civic taking up two spots! I could squeeze in if he weren't parked like a dork."

"Push it," suggested Nate.

Spencer didn't want to risk a scratch on his car. He turned into Willa's street, circled the block again, and finally found a spot.

Nate's brow was beaded with sweat and Spencer's cheeks bright pink when Mrs. Matthews opened the door. There were awkward apologies, brief introductions, and stiff handshakes. A snowy white cloth covered the table laid with ornate china, shining silverware, and crystal glasses. Judge Matthews carved the turkey and Mrs. Matthews invited everyone to help themselves to the pumpkin soup, wild rice, green beans flavored with just a hint of smoked ham, baked stuffed sweet potatoes, corn muffins, cranberry sauce, fresh green salad, and "a perfectly roasted bird." She warned them to save room for her heavenly pecan pie.

Dinner conversation got off to a tense start. Judge Matthews named prominent Fletcher alumni he knew and insisted on the importance of choosing a college that attracted the right kind of people. Willa said the right kind of people were people who cared about others, not future corporate slaves. He asked if she was referring to the whining social workers and naive public defenders that paraded before him to plead the cause of hard-luck hoodlums and cold-blooded killers. Jeannette remarked that a negative environment could make someone choose a negative path. When the judge snorted and said, "Nonsense," Mrs. Matthews quickly offered everyone more muffins and asked Spencer if he knew what college he'd be attending.

"Harvard. My dad went there and my two older brothers."

"A *very* good choice," said the Harvard Law alum, nodding with approval. "We're hoping Willa will smell the Ivy too. And you, Nathaniel?"

Nate snatched the napkin from his lap and wiped his lips.

"I haven't decided yet, but I'm only a junior so I have time."

"Maybe you'll follow in your father's footsteps too, or are you a rebel like Willa?"

Nate smiled, not responding.

"Where *did* your parents go to college, Nathaniel?" asked Mrs. Matthews in the sweetest, most unconcerned voice she could muster. She thought she'd noticed *looks* passing between him and Willa.

"Mom!"

Nate sat upright. "They didn't go to college. My father's an amazing mechanic who can fix anything on any kind of car—American, Japanese, whatever. And Mom helps out old people and people who are alone and too sick to take care of themselves."

Willa's father raised his eyebrows and shot a look at

his wife, who said, "*Ohhh*, one of those home care workers. They're *so* important these days, what with our aging population. Something *else* to be thankful for, dear"—she smiled at her husband—"that we'll never need one because our loving daughter's going to take care of her elderly parents, aren't you, Willa?"

Willa grunted, "Uh-huh," and plunged her knife into a meaty portion of turkey. She felt so bad for Nate, having to say what his parents did in front of everybody.

She wasn't the only one feeling pissed off. Nate heard the subtle snide tone in their voices and resented them for it. He heard his father's saying—a lot of bourgeois black folks value only one color and it ain't black, it's cash green.

"My parents didn't go to college, but I'm really proud of them. Dad works hard six days a week and Mom helps somebody every day she goes to work."

"I hear *that*," said Jeannette, reaching the outer limit of her capacity for *stuck-up*. Willa was cool but her parents, *damn*. "At least you have parents who live together and work. I don't even know who my trifling folks *are*. But looking around at who's raising whom in my projects, maybe it's better that way."

"Oh! Willa didn't mention that you're *also* from—" began Mrs. Matthews.

"The hood? Straight out, yes I am," she added, deliberately adopting her project persona, "all the way *live*." She was enjoying the moment.

Knowing that Jeannette had his back, Nate added, "Having a certain title or a big bank account doesn't make you superior. Being a good person does, and respecting where you came from and the people who're still there. That's what I admire more than . . . trappings."

The judge's mouth moved as if to speak, then was still. Mrs. Matthews adjusted her earring. Jeannette dabbed her mouth with her napkin to cover a faint smile. Spencer smoothed his tie.

"Me too," said Willa, with a defiant glance at her father.

Mrs. Matthews raised her glass. "Then let's all drink a Thanksgiving toast to all the do-gooders of the world!"

The sound of clinking glasses covered the snorting noise Judge Matthews made. Mrs. Matthews recounted the celebrities she met at the Plaza during *Ebony* magazine's Actuaries Star Salute. Judge Matthews described "egregious" examples of revolving-door justice and boasted about cases where, despite the "shackles" judges have to deal with, he was able to give a defendant his "just deserts." The teenagers chewed and listened politely, tapping each other's feet under the table.

By the time everyone was eating pecan pie, the atmosphere had lightened considerably. Spencer told them about his mother's cursed obsession with visiting every Guggenheim museum in the world because she sat on the board.

"Why cursed?" asked Mrs. Matthews, always happy to hear something negative about anyone with more money than her.

"She's cursed because something always goes wrong. Probably since deep down she doesn't even like art and just does the board thing for show."

"I'm a Jacob Lawrence man myself," said the judge, eating a peach since his weight put the pie off-limits, doctor's orders. "As for the rest of it, I call it self-indulgent scrawl."

"My folks have a big Jacob Lawrence poster on the wall of their bedroom," said Nate with a smile.

"Really? Good taste," responded the judge. "Our original *Bar 'n' Grill* piece is on loan to the Harvard's Fogg Museum. It's of Harlem in the thirties. A good place back then."

"And now," said Nate.

Jeannette preferred Basquiat. "His paintings are colorful and have words and signs in them that give them a kind of graffiti flava. He tried to break down stereotypes about black art. Really hip. I saw the movie."

"Basket? Never heard of him. But I'll tell you one

thing, those so-called graffiti artists don't like to come into my courtroom, that's for sure."

Mrs. Matthews *had* heard of the artist.

"Wasn't he . . . *with* . . . Andy Warhol?" she said with a grimace. "And he OD'd on drugs, am I right? Young too." Her grimace deepened.

"So, Spencer, you were saying about your mother . . ." interjected Willa.

"Just that my mother drags us to these places and it's always some kind of disaster. The Guggenheim in Venice was flooded the day we went. Did you know Peggy Guggenheim is buried with a whole kennel of her beloved dogs, and their names are engraved on the same tombstone as hers?"

The whole table laughed.

"Another time she took us to Bilbao in Spain, but the Basque separatists had phoned in a bomb threat to the museum and it was being evacuated just as our driver pulled up. Then there was the time the dinky little one in Berlin was closed the day we showed up and she got the manager's phone number to demand he open it for a private visit, but whoever answered only spoke German."

"Or maybe they just pretended," said Nate.

"That's what I think. But the craziest time was when we went to the one in the Venetian Casino in Las Vegas and all these drunk gamblers were staggering around laughing at the paintings and bumping into people. Actually, that was the most fun I ever had at a museum."

"Sounds like she should just stick to New York," said Willa.

Judge Matthews excused himself from the table to go smoke his pipe on the terrace. Mrs. Matthews told the teens to relax and enjoy themselves, and began clearing the table. Jeannette jumped up to help but was turned down. The foursome plopped down on the thick carpet in the salon and played cards, gossiped about teachers and kids, and flipped through the Matthewses' photo albums, hooting at every shot of Willa as a skinny, woolly-headed little girl. Spencer loosened his tie and coughed two times, the ready-to-leave signal they'd agreed upon. Thanksgiving at the Matthewses' ended for the boys with the same awkward handshakes that began it. Jeannette was spending the night.

"How are you two getting back to wherever you're going?" asked Judge Matthews, who had come out of his study to say good night. "Train?"

"We're going back up to school—lots of work," said Spencer. "I have my car."

"Car? At your age? Do you have a license?"

Spencer grinned guiltily. He'd meant to get one but who needed the hassle? Besides, he had a permit.

Judge Matthews sensed the answer to his question. "I hope you have a licensed driver with you." He glanced skeptically at Nate. "Unlicensed driving is a serious offense."

Spencer remembered a restaurant they'd seen on the way. "I know, sir. That's why I'm picking up my older brother at the Kafka Café right down the road. Thanks again for a wonderful dinner."

The cold air and dark night made them giddy. They made a racket out on the street with their howls of laughter and merciless impressions of their hosts. What bores! declared Spencer. How stuck-up! exclaimed Nate. Poor Willa! they said.

"The line about the trappings of respectability was perfect! You saw the look on his face?"

Nate shook his head. "So what, he went to Harvard, big deal. I bet he never stopped to help someone whose car broke down."

"Oh, I'm sure he stopped, but probably to make a citizen's arrest for blocking traffic so he could give them their *just deserts*. Which, by the way, were great."

"Yeah, but my mom's pie is better. Even though she *is* just a home care worker."

Now Spencer shook his head. "My parents are complete snobs too, but at least they're classy enough to hide it until the guests have left. So do your folks really have one of those paintings by that artist he likes, Lawrence something?"

"Hell, no. I just wanted to mess with Mr. Judge."

Spencer chuckled. "I had a feeling . . ."

They climbed into Spencer's car with full stomachs and rowdy spirits. The expressway was wide open and Spencer tested the snazzy little car's pickup, singing along to Coldplay. Nate rocked in his seat, enjoying the night. Willa had been right about her parents. He *didn't* like them. But he sure liked her.

They'd been driving about a half hour when Spencer spotted a state patrol car in a wooded copse. Before he could slow down, the vehicle had swerved onto the expressway, lights flashing.

"Bummer! The police!" said Spencer.

Nate's heart jumped. The police. One of the worst announcements a black teenager could hear. His mind flew to friends beaten, cuffed, even shot, some guilty, others not. He flashed on his mother, his dad, Eli. They'd be destroyed. Spencer was the one speeding with no license, but Nate felt that the patrolman's wrath would for some reason crash down on *him*.

The wheels of the Karmann-Ghia crunched gravel as Spencer slowed to a stop on the shoulder of the road and shut off the music. The patrolman left the car lights flashing and approached on the driver's side, holding a long black flashlight.

"Good evening."

"Good evening," responded Spencer pleasantly. "Is there a problem?"

"Indeed there is. Doing seventy miles an hour in a fifty-five zone. Let's see your license and registration, please."

As Spencer fumbled in the glove compartment a beam of light hit Nate in the face.

"Good evening, fella."

"Good evening, officer." Nate felt his throat tighten with each syllable.

Spencer handed over the documents, explaining that they'd been at a Thanksgiving dinner for Fletcher's senior class, and his older brother who'd driven them there drank too much and got sick, but luckily he had his permit and . . .

The patrolman pointed the beam at Nate's blazer pocket, lighting up the Fletcher crest.

"You at Fletcher too?"

"Yeah," responded Nate, then corrected himself. "Yes."

The man eyed Nate. "You twenty-one or older and the holder of a valid driver's license?"

"No. Sir."

He looked over the paperwork and told Spencer that a smart kid like himself should know better than to speed, and certainly not with a learner's permit. Spencer said he was really sorry, his parents were away in Europe, and he panicked when they took his brother to the hospital and . . .

"I'm giving you a warning this time. But you can't drive this car on that permit without the presence of a licensed driver twenty-one years of age or older. Have a good one, gentlemen."

"Happy Thanksgiving, sir!" said Spencer as the patrolman walked back to his car.

Spencer put the music back on. He said a lot of people have the wrong idea about cops, that they can be really cool if you know how to talk to them. Raskolnikov would've choked, he smirked, thinking back to Nate's novel. He drove fast, singing and humming. Nate felt nauseous the whole ride back.

Students returned to campus after Thanksgiving break and hunkered down for the grim stretch that separated one holiday from the next. The sky was barely light when morning alarms would buzz and darkened before classes ended. The ambitious kids hotdogged in the front rows, trying to nudge up their grade point average by raising their hands every two minutes. Others slumped in the rear of the classrooms, doodling, writing each other notes, or making Christmas lists.

Nate's thoughts were on Willa when suddenly she appeared before him in the hall.

"Hey, I was just thinking about you."

She smiled. "Why?"

He faltered. Any other girl would've said something like "Really? What were you thinking?" Maybe even blushed a little. Something about Willa's responses always threw him off.

"Why? Uh, because . . . I wanted to say thanks for having me and Spencer over at Thanksgiving."

"You already did. A few times." She shifted her books from one arm to the other.

He remembered one of Hustle's lectures about dealing with shorties. Nah, he couldn't keep letting this *female* make him squirm like a punk. He flexed his broad chest. "Yeah, I know. The other thing was that I have an extra ticket for a special amateur show they're doing at the Apollo in a couple of weeks. I figured we could . . ." Again, his nerves got the best of him. "I mean, I was gonna invite you. You know, it would just be for the day, after morning classes."

For once, and much to his relief, she didn't pierce him with a long gaze. "*Harlem*, cool. I've wanted to visit *forever* but felt it would be better if I went with someone *from* there, you know . . . a native, instead of going by myself. We live so close, but my parents always say Harlem's too . . ."

"Dangerous? That's bogus. People talk like you can't walk down the street without being robbed. We have the same bad stuff that goes on anywhere—it *is* New York. But Harlem's just people living—working, playing, going to church, taking care of their families. There are restaurants, parks, all kinds of stores and shops, famous landmark buildings . . . Anyhow, just think about it."

"I will," she said, already doing exactly that. "I will."

Snowflakes fell sparkling and powdery from high above sky-scrapers, landing in mounds and thawing slowly into streams of dull, icy slush. Children, shoppers, office workers, tourists, and police moved in slow motion through the wintry congestion. Nate and Willa inched their way towards the famous Apollo marquee. Willa had been animated on the train ride down, reliving Furies victories, describing her favorite music videos, joking about teachers, and criticizing her parents. Once in the city, however, she grew quiet and watchful. Nate was still in his school clothes and acutely aware of it. The crowd shivered and shouted outside the theater.

"It's cold! Y'all *needs* to open up them doors, I can't feel my feets!"

"Bootaytay, over here! You *know* you see me! Over *here*, stupid!"

"Omigod, I can't believe I'm standing outside the Apollo Theater, totally in the middle of Harlem. Too exciting!"

A hustler walked up to the suburban-looking young couple. " 'Sup, dawg, y'all need tickets? Got front row for twenty-fo'."

Nate sent the scalper on his way. They had front-row seats and he hadn't paid twenty-four dollars for them either. The doors swung open and the chilly crowd bustled inside.

People jostled one another in front of the coat check.

"You checking your coat?" asked Nate.

Willa hugged her Venus Williams Collection quilted leather jacket close to her body, shaking her head no.

"Me neither. It gets too jammed up after the show. Let's go see the Wall of Fame," he said proudly. He pushed his way across the lobby. "Look at all the people who got their start right here!" They were directly in front of the photo collage. "You probably already know about the oldies like Billie Holiday and James Brown and Lionel Hampton, but check *them* out!" He pointed to five boys, all smiles and afros. "The Jackson 5. That's Michael at nine."

Willa blinked. "He's so cute! I didn't know he ever looked . . . normal." She stepped up close to the photo of a little girl. "Is *that* Stephanie Mills?! Jeannette *loves* her. She won amateur night at eleven years old?! I'm impressed."

Nate showed her star after star—Sarah Vaughn, Marvin Gaye, The Supremes, Aretha Franklin, Stevie Wonder, Brandy, Prince, even Tony Bennett. Each one touched by *his* neighborhood, Harlem, USA. He told her how a Jewish family, the Schiffmans, owned the Apollo for forty years and nurtured the careers of tons of unknowns who later became legends. It had gotten a little run-down lately, but the Apollo was coming back. Definitely.

"You're really into this place, huh?" asked Willa, a warm look in her eyes.

"I guess I'm just into Harlem. We're always getting dissed, but there's a lot that's great about it."

They took their seats in the cavernous theater, and the world's rowdiest talent show began. The emcee first welcomed "all the Japanese in the house."

"I know y'all scared. Lemme hear ya say '*Haay-elp!*'" he sang out.

He stuck the mic in the air. The group giggled, nodding rapidly.

"Say 'Help, help, help!'"

The rest of the audience chanted with him.

"*Arigato,*" he said, thanking them with a slight bow.

The tourists applauded wildly at the sound of a word

in their own language. He thanked them for coming in their military convoy.

"With all them armored buses lined up bumper to bumper out there, Harlem got its *own* missile defense shield."

Laughter filled the room.

"Now, we got a great show today, and *pleeeze* . . . try to have *some* pity on the performers 'cause they is *truly* pitiful! Nah! Nah! That was a joke. There is *nothin'* backstage but talent and *mo'* talent. And my seventy-year-old mama . . . But she just sweepin' up. *One* of us gots to get paid!"

He paused for people to catch their breath and wipe the tears of laughter from their eyes. Willa was holding her sides.

"This is great, Nathaniel! Thank you for bringing me. He's so funny, he should be on Mad TV!"

"So listen up," the emcee continued. "Y'all heard what happened last Father's Day, right? Florists all over Harlem went *wild*, rioting in the streets 'cause they didn't make a damn *penny*. Harlem kids was like, Father's Day? Only father I got up there artin' in Heaven. Man, a lot of folks think them flower-shop homeys be soft but they don't *play*. They was attacking brothers who looked like they was even *thinking* 'bout doin' the quick hit lickety-split. Whole *tribes* of 'em was on the rampage, wieldin' tulips like clubs, jabbing long-stemmed roses in the air, throwing chocolates. Some was even swingin' baby trees!"

The whole theater thundered with howls and screams.

"It ain't funny, y'all, it was like *Nightmare on a Hundred Twenty-fifth Street*! They'd swarm and interrogate a brother like them Homeland Security dudes: 'How many kids you got? What they names? What they five mamas' names? They git you anything last year? No?! Why the hell not! What you mean, they ain't never *met* you?!' Then they'd beat him *down*, man, scratch him up bad with rose thorns!"

A tidal wave of foot stomping and clapping washed through the theater.

"Thank you, thank you. Y'all a great audience. Now, we holding this special amateur night at noontime instead of in the evening like we usually do 'cause it's that time of the month . . . No, ladies, not *that* time, although now that I think about it, I *do* feel kinda moody . . . It's *rent* time, and we gotta jet before the landlord show up for his money!"

The first contestant stepped onstage and got off to a very bad start the moment he touched the Apollo's lucky Tree of Hope.

"That hair need more than luck!" yelled a woman in the audience.

The lights went down and the crooner closed his

eyes. When he began, the mic was too close to his mouth, which created harsh feedback.

"Myyy funny Valentiiiine . . ."

"Aaiiieeee!"

"Owwww!"

"Turn that noise down!"

"Sweeeet funny Valentiiiine . . ."

Despite having once been home to the likes of Nat "King" Cole and Sammy Davis Jr., the Apollo was no longer a place for crooners. Rhythm and blues, yes. Gospel, yes. Hip-hop, yes. "My Funny Valentine," no. Grumbling grew into catcalls which mushroomed into the boos that brought out the colorful dancing clown with his clanging bell to escort the singer off the stage.

"Harlem don't play," boasted Nate.

"I *see*," said Willa. "That was brutal."

Next out were four skinny sisters who looked like they were all still in elementary school. They threw their big hearts and little voices into a frenzied version of the gospel hit "Oh Happy Day" and brought cheers from the crowd, as much renowned for its generosity with children as for its merciless treatment of adults.

Two Black Chicks Bitchin' joked about people with ashy knees, recipes for hot grits that spread smoothly on the backs of unfaithful boyfriends, stank booty thong dancers in music videos, R. Kelly singing "I Believe I Can Lie," and Condoleezza Rice's hairdo. The audience enjoyed them.

During the intermission, Willa bought Apollo caps and sweatshirts for herself, Jeannette, and her parents. The show's second half began with a hefty diva strutting onto the stage. Spilling over the top of her low-cut, clingy red gown, she unleashed pandemonium with the boom of her husky voice and the swing of her ample figure.

"*What you want!*" she offered, her hand outstretched to every man in the room.

"Don't hurt nobody, girl!"

"*Baby, I got it!*" she declared, her hips gyrating.

"Oh man! Heh, heh, I hear that!"

"*What you need!*" she wailed, writhing and sliding her hand over her bosom.

The crowd roared, shouted, and barked.

"*You know I got it!*" she moaned, bending her knees and repeatedly arching her back.

By the time she got around to saying that what she *really* wanted was a little respect, Willa was scowling. Nate was bobbing his head and dancing in his seat.

"*Jeeeez*, how tacky. You *like* her?"

"Unh-unh, not really," he said. "I just like the song."

Willa smirked. "Yeah, sure. And you're staring at her

cheap necklace, right? Are you gonna start barking too, like the rest of the kennel?"

Nate struggled to hold it in but laughter burst out. He loved her sarcasm. He loved her prim and proper attitude. She was so different from other girls he knew. At that moment her eyes caught a ray of spotlight and suddenly reflected a soft emerald. He loved them too. Before he had even weighed the pros and cons, he'd kissed her on the lips. She just looked at him. A second before he was about to say sorry, she gave him a smile.

The rest of the show passed in a wild tumult of boos, applause, hisses, and barks that championed or condemned rappers, comics, dancers, gospel singers, ventriloquists, and poets. At the end of the afternoon, it was a pair of sexy-voiced teenage twins who'd wobbled their heads and rolled their eyes through "The Boy Is Mine" who won.

Still buzzing, the satisfied audience pushed towards the lobby. Nate was behind Willa, his hands on both her shoulders, when he felt a tug on his arm. He turned and found himself facing Hustle.

"Wassup, Schoolie! I *thought* that was you I seen from the balcony. My dawgs Hydro and Ride somewhere around here." Hustle shouted over the heads of the crowd. "Yo, Hydro! Ride! Double Fo'?! Where my dawgs at? Schoolie's up in here!"

Hustle's Brotherhood crew shoved their way towards Nate. Willa recoiled. Black do-rags covered their heads, and their clothes swallowed them. They had bloodshot eyes and heavy lids.

Hydro kept swallowing as if he had cotton in his mouth. "Schoolie. Wassup. Good to see you, I gotta get me something to drink."

Ride was either rubbing or picking his nose, Willa wasn't sure which. He and Nate locked hands and shoulder hugged. "You saw that show?! That shit was *hype*," said Ride.

Double Fo's head bobbed up and down. "Yeah, man, and the hoochie in red . . . Damn!"

Hustle examined Nate's clothes. "What's with the Tiger Woods look? Shorty here dressin' you?" He flashed his slip-on gold front tooth at Willa in a wide smile. "Don't hold out on a good brother now, who the hottie?"

Nate made a quick introduction.

"This is Willa, a friend from school. Willa, Hustle . . . a neighbor."

She shuddered and forced out a very dry "Hi."

"I'm fiendin' on *that*, boyee," he said to Nate, staring at Willa.

Nate took Willa's hand and began moving towards the exit. "Okay, Hustle, see ya later."

"Ah-ight, homey. Holla atcha boy if you wanna hang, you know where I be." He ran his eyes over her body. "Bye-bye . . . *Willa.*"

Like a fullback, Nate shouldered a path through the throng. He had hoped they could visit his neighborhood and later drop by and say hello to his parents before catching the train back. As soon as they were on the street, Willa freed her hand.

"*Who* was *that?*"

Her superior tone irked him.

"Eric. We call him Hustle."

She raised her eyebrows. "We? Who's we? You and Hydro and Ride and Double Po'? Don't *any* of your friends have normal names?"

"Double *Fo'.*"

"Pardon me, Double *Fo'.* And I suppose that stands for two four's as in forty-four magnum?"

"Very *good*, Miss Inwood," said Nate, instantly regretting his sarcasm.

"Very trite, actually. Every boy-in-the-hood movie has some loser named for a gun."

He tried to lighten things up. "These are the guys I grew up with, Willa. Friends. They're the Brotherhood and they protect our block. What's the problem?"

They were almost at 128th Street.

"You're asking *me* what's the problem? Why don't you ask your gangsta Brotherhood friend what is *his* problem? First of all, I'm a person and I don't like being discussed like a . . . thing . . . when I'm standing right there. And I *don't* appreciate being referred to as a hottie, shorty, or whatever dumb word you and *ya boys* use."

She stopped walking.

"Why don't you just chill out, Willa. *What* is the big deal? This is Harlem, okay? Not snotty Inwood. People are real here and they talk how they talk and they got the names they got. Come on, we're having a good time and I want to show you more of Harlem, introduce you to my folks. Don't go drama on me."

She imitated his voice. "*Why don't you just chill out . . . Don't go drama on me.* You sound just *like* them. And what is so *real* about wearing pants that are falling off and speaking bad English? Do your hoodlum friends go to school? Do they have futures? You know what, Nathaniel, I'm beginning to realize that I don't know you very well at all . . . *Schoolie*. And you know what else? I think I've seen more than enough of your Harlem *and* your homeys."

As if she had willed it, a gypsy cab pulled up at the corner and let out a passenger. Willa threw up her hand.

"Taxi!"

Nate watched the taxi disappear down the boulevard. He didn't know if he was angrier at her or Hustle or himself. It wasn't Hustle's fault. They were friends, and no prissy bourgeois girl was going to change that. The sudden memory of the kiss and her smile sent an ache through his stomach. Oh forget her, with those weird eyes. She was too complicated, too emotional, too hard to read. He had Shantay anyway, simple and laid back, like in the LL Cool J song, a "round-the-way girl." He thought about surprising her, but she'd be in school on a Wednesday afternoon. Maybe if he ran back to the Apollo he might catch up with Hustle and the crew. They were probably long gone. It was too cold to cruise the streets. He could just go back to school. Maybe he'd be on the same train as Willa. No, he was home and his folks would want to see him. He'd wait and surprise *them*.

The apartment was nice and warm. He tossed his jacket on the couch. It smelled like home. He heard faint music coming from the hallway. Eli was famous for leaving things on—the TV, radios. Once he even left on the oven. Luckily, it was empty. Nate went to turn off the radio in his room. He opened the door and found his brother and a girl wrapped around each other in bed, their naked shoulders visible. Half a bottle of beer was on the dresser next to an ashtray of cigarette butts and a roach clip.

Eli rose onto an elbow, the lids of his pink eyes

half-closed. His bare chest blocked Nate's view of the girl.

"*Daaammn*, what you doin' home?" slurred Eli.

"Who dat?" drawled the girl.

Nate knew the voice. Shantay. The air left his lungs. The muscles in his neck clenched. The strength drained from his legs.

He glared at Eli. "You bastard."

He pounced on his brother, snatched him from the bed, and threw him completely across the room. Eli slammed against the wall with a loud moan and lay naked on the floor. Shantay stared at Nate as if from atop a faraway peak, narrowing her eyes to bring the distant object into focus. He couldn't look at her at all.

Dusk whipped up a cold wind. Slush hardened into ice. Traffic lights switched from green to red. The chill of the air wasn't felt on his skin. Rush-hour sounds seemed not to reach his ears. He walked, seeing only what wasn't there. Emerald eyes. Parted lips. Quilted black leather. An ashtray. Shoulders. A horn honked.

"Watch where you going, brother," called a man from the curb Nate had just stepped off. "That car almost hit you."

Nate kept walking, against the strong wind. He liked the effort and struggle, the fight it took to move forward. He saw a street sign. He wasn't far from Randall's place.

"Well, look what the cat dragged— Are you okay? You look dreadful . . . and frozen. Come inside." Randall was still in a business suit. Kenny was at the office. "Your eyes are all . . . Have you been crying? Give me your jacket."

Nate followed him to the kitchen. "It's freezing out there. I just put on some water. You want tea? Earl Grey? Mint? You look like you need mint."

They sat in silence, stirring honey into the tea.

"Nate, I've been your adviser but I also consider myself a friend. You can talk to me. Is it school? Did you fail something? You're not on probation, are you?"

Nate shook his head. How could he tell Randy? A guy like *that* wouldn't understand. He wished he hadn't ended up there.

"I gotta go. Thanks for the tea." He slid off the stool.

"Is it police trouble?"

"Nah. Forget it, I shouldn't have come. I was just walking wherever."

Randall stood too. "Okay, fine. You want to go, then go. But I worked damned hard to help you get where you are today, and if something's gone wrong I feel I deserve to know about it."

Nate sat down. Where would he go anyway? Home, to act like everything was fine? To school to look for Willa, who probably hated him? Back out in the cold? Things were going so good, then the script flipped.

"It's a girl problem, Randall. You wouldn't get it."

"Oh I wouldn't? You think I've never had a girl-friend? I have. You think girl problems are that different from boy problems? They're not." He thought for a moment. "Unless someone's pregnant. That's it, isn't it? Your girlfriend's pregnant."

"She may be. But not by me."

"Oh boy. That's a hard one. I'm sorry to hear it."

"And if she is, it's by my brother, Eli. I just found them . . ."

"What? Jeez . . . for crying out loud. Eli?" Randall ran out of words. He put the teapot and cups on a tray. "Let's go in the living room. I think we need to be where it's a *lot* more comfortable."

Nate slumped onto a chair, and out poured the whole story—Willa, the Apollo, Hustle, Eli and Shantay. He was angry at Shantay even though they had agreed that they could each go out with other people. But couldn't she have found someone besides his own brother? And how long had they been hanging out? He recalled how often she couldn't see him or cut short *their* time to-gether to meet this girlfriend or keep that appointment.

The times she didn't answer her phone. But Eli was the one he hated. His big brother, the one he worried about, the one who was probably laughing at him while he . . .

"It's like I can't believe what I saw, but I can't stop seeing it either." Maybe that was his punishment for going after Willa.

"You're sixteen, unmarried, childless, and free to go after any girl, anybody you choose. You're not the one in the wrong here. Eli is."

Nate made Randall promise not to tell anyone—not his folks, not Kenny, nobody.

It was well into evening when Kenny arrived home. After playfully harassing Nate about a hip-hop tape he'd promised to send but didn't, Kenny declared he was absolutely famished. Neither man felt like cooking, and Nate didn't want to go out. So Randall picked up the phone.

Within twenty minutes they were seated at the dining room table, breathing in the rich aromas of Thai spring rolls, sautéed string beans, barbecued shrimp, and charbroiled chicken. The architects discussed clients and drawings while Nate moved food around the plate with his fork.

"You're not eating!" exclaimed Kenny. "Two spring rolls are not enough for a lacrosse killing machine. At Dartmouth I was a ferocious defender, did Randall tell you? 'The Asian Assassin' was my name."

"How racist," said Randall. "That's like calling someone 'The Mighty Whitey.' "

"I know, but they feared me. I would eat guys like Nathaniel for appetizers . . . You play midfield, right? Then I'd wait for the main course, the hunky attackers. *Grrrrr . . .*"

"*Kenny* . . . I think Nathaniel's tired and may not be very hungry."

Nate looked at his watch. Maybe he could crash at the place where Hustle stayed.

Randall covered Nate's Timex with his hand. "Don't even think about leaving. It's past eleven, the ice age has returned, and your eyes are drooping. There are four bedrooms here and you're sleeping in one of them tonight."

Nate didn't protest. He was too tired.

A narrow band of sunlight spilled through a slit between the window drapes. He didn't recognize his bedroom. His thighs were as heavy as tree trunks. His head hurt. His throat felt sore. Distant bells of a clock chimed quietly. He wasn't *in* his bedroom. A cargo ship on the Hudson River blew its horn. Nate pulled back the curtain and looked out onto a choppy river carrying chunks of floating ice and wide ships. In the park, skinny tree branches were encased in icicles, and clumps of snow sat on bushes. Cars sped up and down wet, black streets. He sneezed. A chill shook his body.

The bedroom had its own bathroom and Nate lingered in the shower, changing the water flow back and forth from a pounding single stream to a gentle rainfall. A multitude of mirrors reflected him wrapped in a thick white terrycloth bathrobe and matching slippers. He opened the door. A folded note dropped to the floor.

Good morning! Help yourself to anything in the kitchen. Stay as long as you like. The front door locks automatically when you shut it. Keep me posted.

Randy

Early lunchgoers were dashing into restaurants. Nate's cell-phone battery was low and he had a hard time hearing Hustle over the street noises.

"Where?!" asked Nate loudly. "Forty-deuce and *where?!* I can hardly hear you, man."

They agreed to meet in Times Square, at an apartment Hustle used to stash store merchandise. Shoppers, hawkers, tourists, and scores of working New Yorkers waded and stepped through slushy intersections and busy streets. Giant billboards towered and blinked, news bars ran round and round buildings with the latest headlines and stock market numbers. Nate found his way to 47th Street, passing a crowd gathered to watch dancing Santas.

Hustle spotted him. " 'Sup, dawg?! Now ain't this something, Schoolie playing hooky. I see you ain't changed your clothes, so I know you wasn't home. You and . . . what was her name? A weird name . . . oh yeah, Willa . . . coulda stayed at my crib, ya know."

Willa. The very word cut. Nate managed a smirky smile.

"It wasn't even like that, I put her behind on the next train outta Harlem. She was steady sweatin' me. You tripped her out the way you talked to her. She didn't 'preciate it."

No way was he gonna tell Mr. Ladies' Man that he was the one ditched by the girl he wanted or that Eli was doing the girl he had.

Hustle nodded as though he understood perfectly. "I hear that. I woulda done likewise, even though she was fine. Them high-strung, upscale hotties be bringing mad stress. So why you didn't go home?"

Nate said he was hanging with a couple of his boys over by Convent Park. He left it at that. Yesterday was the last place he wanted to dwell.

"So hook me up with some gear, Hustle, or you wanna roll with me dressed like this?"

The shabby room looked like a warehouse instead of somebody's studio apartment. Everywhere there were stacks and piles of designer suits and shirts, coats and jackets made from every fabric, jeans and dresses of all colors, shoes and sneakers for every occasion. Every item with a price tag still on and most of them bearing theft-proof security devices.

"You right," said Hustle, laughing. "You puttin' a hurt on my eyes with the schoolboy rags. Borrow whatever you want. *Borrow*."

Nate outfitted himself in Projectboy clothing, a pair of Urban Sole boots, and a black FUBU down coat with fake fur trim.

Hustle approved. "Now you comin' *correct*, my man."

Nate was curious about Hustle's operation. "Why's all your stuff in here? Whose place is this?"

Hustle said he couldn't be running up to Harlem after every boost. So he paid a dude called Montana, a business associate who owned the empty apartment, to let him drop merchandise there. "For extra, he'll run me to a customer's crib in his Jeep, but he won't go uptown. Scared. He a white dude. Now let's eat; there's a White Castle right near here."

At the restaurant, they stuffed themselves with mushy square hamburgers and greasy french fries. Afterwards, it was off to VideoRama. The game parlor was packed. Hustle bought a bunch of tokens and found his favorite machine. He pointed his plastic gun at the screen and total war broke out. Masked men fell one after another before his deadly aim. Nate dropped in his token, picked up his weapon, and began firing as well. By the time "Game Over" flashed on both screens for the umpteenth time, the two had exploded several desert safe houses, blown up scores of mountain caves, and massacred hundreds of members of the Evil Terror Network.

As they were leaving, Hustle said he had some business to take care of uptown for a friend with Dominican trouble. "A numbers turf war. You know how that be, them Dominicans muscling in on my dawg's territory. Ride with me, Schoolie, I could use some eyes watching my back."

"Ride?" asked Nate. "Since when you got wheels?"

"Since I pay Montana to let me borrow his to make deliveries or take merchandise to my crib uptown. Or for other stuff."

The whole deal sounded like bad news to Nate. He'd made it this far in life without getting into any real trouble or being locked up like most of his friends, including Hustle, who'd been busted a few times but always managed to slip through the system's cracks. What was this "business" Hustle had to take care of that needed a lookout?

"What you gonna be gettin' into? I'm a schoolboy, you know," said Nate only half jokingly.

"And that don't call you a punk, right? Ain't that what you always say? Come on, Schoolie, hold me down with this. I'ma mess up they office a little to send them a message. Nobody's gon' get hurt or nothing. They be on the street most of the time anyway, so it ain't like we—I mean *I'm*—gonna meet no resistance, know what I'm sayin'? Come on, Nate? I'll let you keep everything you wearing."

Hustle only called him "Nate" when he really wanted something. Nate didn't want to go. But his emotions were outrunning his reason. This was so messed up anyway. Why the hell not.

"Okay, I'll roll with you, but no drama."

"Ah-ight, that's my dawg! All you gotta do is sit in the Jeep and wait for me to come out. I'ma be right on the first floor. If anything pops off suspicious, whistle or something."

Hustle jimmied open the door to the musty apartment. Plaster peels and a bare lightbulb dangled from the ceiling. A wooden desk and chair, a rotary telephone, a stained couch, and a file cabinet. He sliced open the couch and pulled out its stuffing, beat the chair against the walls until it broke, used one of the legs to break windows, tore the phone cord from the wall, and dumped the contents of the file cabinet across the floor. He put a cigarette lighter to pages of handwritten records, notebooks, and various papers. The job was done, the place thoroughly trashed. Jazzed by the rush of violence, he ran from the building grinning and pumping his fist in the air. Nate was waiting in the driver's seat when Hustle leapt into the car. "Drive, man!" Nate drove off, his head pounding and his stomach in knots.

The red Jeep was cruising at normal speed down Central Park West. The CD player was blasting when Black Rob's voice was suddenly drowned out by the squeal of a siren. Lights reflecting in the rearview mirror flashed into Nate's eyes. At first he thought, or rather he made himself hope, that it was a fire engine. It wasn't. Cops. What was he going to do? His folks didn't even know he was in the city, and now he was about to be busted for *Hustle's* break-in. He *knew* he shouldn't have gone, he *felt* it. It was beginning to seem like Hustle brought him a steady stream of bad luck. Mom, Dad, Randy, Mrs. Quilly . . . this would break their hearts. How could he have been so stupid, put so much at risk? Eli was the one with the inmate future, not him! And Willa . . . Getting suspended from school and put in prison would confirm her worst thoughts about him.

Hustle spun around. "Awww *man*! You straight, right? You got a license? 'Cause I don't."

Nate flicked on the turn signal and eased the Jeep over to the curb. He thought back to Thanksgiving and Spencer's Karmann-Ghia.

"I got a permit—hopefully, that'll be cool. The registration's in there, right?" He pointed to the glove compartment, his voice cracking just slightly when he said "right?"

"It *betta* be," answered Hustle, reaching inside.

Nate rolled down his window. Two cops moved towards the car, one on each side.

"Put your hands where I can see them!" shouted the one nearest Hustle.

The other cop stood back and slightly to the rear. "You live around here?" he asked, shining his light in the back seat and on the floor.

"No, sir, we're on our way downtown," said Nate.

"Yeah, we got people waitin' for us and we in a hurry," added Hustle.

"Nobody's talking to you, buddy. I'm talking to your friend right now." He directed his request to Nate. "Lemme see your license and registration."

Hustle sucked his teeth loud. "That's exactly what I was reaching for when your partner here told me to put my hands—"

"Look, you," interrupted the partner. "I said shut up already. Freddy, check motormouth's ID."

Officer Freddy Rostino took Hustle's identification card and returned to the patrol car, where he plugged the information into the vehicle's computer.

Nate swallowed. "Is it okay if I go in my back pocket?"

"Sure, buddy, if that's where your license is."

Hustle couldn't sit still. "Look, man, what we do? What's the charges"—he read the man's badge—"Officer Nelson?"

"You just can't keep that mouth shut, can you? What your friend here did is drive with a broken taillight."

He examined Nate's learner's permit, eyed Nate, then examined it some more. "This car stolen?"

"No, sir, it belongs to a friend of ours."

"It's my—" began Hustle.

Nate elbowed him. Hustle shut up.

The cop looked over the registration papers Nate gave him and handed them back to Nate.

He addressed Hustle. "You got a driver's license?"

"Nah. But I ain't the one drivin' so—"

"Mr. Whitely, this permit does not authorize you to drive without a licensed driver in the car."

Nate prayed for a clever Spencer lie to come to him, but none did. He couldn't even focus his thoughts on the truth.

"Um . . . I . . . We were heading home . . ."

Officer Rostino returned from the patrol car and whispered to his partner, whose body tensed.

"Any guns or weapons in this car?" demanded Officer Nelson.

"No, sir," answered Nate emphatically, his eyes widening.

"Okay," continued the cop. "Now I'm gonna ask both of you to exit the vehicle . . . slowly."

"Awww, come on, man, we ain't done nothin'. Why y'all sweatin' us?!" Hustle was breathing hard.

Once out of the car, they were carefully patted down and quickly put in handcuffs.

Officer Rostino took hold of Hustle's arm as if he expected him to run. "Eric Samson, there's an outstanding warrant for your arrest for petty larceny, larceny, and grand theft. You have the right to remain silent. Anything you say can and will be used against you in a court of law. You have the right to speak to an attorney, and to have an attorney present during any questioning. If you cannot afford a lawyer, one will be appointed to you free of charge."

Hustle groaned. Nate bit his lip. The teens were put in the back seat of the squad car and driven to the police precinct. Montana's red Jeep remained where Nate had stopped it, in a tow-away zone.

In custody Hustle—now called Eric Samson—resembled a scared kid, albeit one in designer gangsta gear. As hardcore as he struggled to appear, the quiver on the lip, the anxious eyes, and the forced defiant gait betrayed him. A table full of detectives were very pleased to make his acquaintance, they joked. Had been looking forward to it for months. There were surveillance tapes from several stores, they said. Did he have inside help? Was Whitely an accomplice? Since Eric wasn't yet seventeen, they offered to call his parents. He said they were dead, and requested a lawyer.

In a separate interrogation room, Nate was shivering and sweating. He'd never before been picked up and questioned. Because of his age, the officers asked for his parents' phone number as well. There was no way he was going to bring his folks into this mess. He wouldn't even be able to say the word . . . *busted*. It would surely kill them on the spot. He said his folks were out of town, and that no, he didn't have a number where they could be reached.

"That's fine by me, my friend," said Detective Salvatore Flick. "But don't turn around and say we didn't try. You want a lawyer too?"

"No. I didn't do anything."

"As you wish."

Flick did most of the talking. He seemed all right. Maybe everything would work out, thought Nate, once he explained that he'd only waited outside the building. *That* wasn't a crime. Nate prepared himself for the questions that would come—who actually entered the apartment, who busted it up, why? But Flick said nothing. So neither did Nate.

Another cop barged into the room.

"His folks been called?" barked lead detective Denton Bavure.

"He doesn't know the phone number," answered Detective Flick.

"Sure. Right." Detective Bavure glared at Nate. "Okay, tough guy, we can do this the easy way or the hard way. It's your choice. Detective Flick here's a softy, but I'm a bastard and I don't got a lotta patience."

Nate's stomach knotted up and his throat tightened. His heart pounded. He imagined Raskolnikov feeling the same way a hundred years ago and acting so guilty that he drew suspicion to him like a magnet. Nate had to hold himself together, do better than a panicky Russian law student. He asked for a cup of water.

"Later," snapped Bavure. He asked Nate's full name, address, date of birth, year in school, and prior arrests. Detective Flick wrote down everything Nate said. Then the serious questioning commenced. And much to Nate's shock, not a word was mentioned about numbers running or Dominicans or vandalism. Detective Bavure kept asking him about "hot merchandise" and "boosting." Were they pretending not to be interested in the break-in to fool him, win his trust, trick him into blabbing something? He wanted to rejoice, yet he was afraid to believe he just might be spared. Because of *that*, he was completely innocent.

"Okay, Nat."

"Nate, sir."

"How long you been boosting, Nat?"

"Sir?"

Bavure banged his fist on the table. "Don't gimme that 'sir' crap! Eric's cooperating to save his own ass. He's already told us how *you* get the clothes out the store and *he* sells them uptown. Now, if that's not how your little operation works, you best start talking fast 'cause you're looking at some hard juvvie-hall time, homey."

Detective Flick slid his chair next to Nate's. "Listen, Nate, I like you. I could tell right off the bat that you were a good kid, not like your punk friend in the next room, who's in there squealing like a mouse on a glue tray. You know what I think?" He looked at his colleague. "Denny, I know you're not with me on this, but I got my own opinion." He looked Nate in the eye. "I think good ol' Eric got you into this and now he's trying to pin the whole rap on you. Come clean with me and I'll talk to the judge, maybe get you off with some counseling, community service, that kind of thing. Life's pretty tough up there in Harlem, I understand that. A guy can fall in with a bad crowd . . . I see it every day. Just work with us. Don't make Dynamite Denny here lose his patience, okay, kid? You don't want that."

Nate knew Hustle would never say what the detectives were claiming he'd say, and in any case Nate had seen enough cop shows on television to recognize the detectives' nice cop / mean cop routine.

"I *am* coming clean with you. I haven't stolen anything or sold anything stolen or anything you're saying. Eric and I played some video games at Times Square and were on our way to the movies, that's all. Then I was going to catch the train and go back upstate to school. I don't steal stuff."

Detective Bavure leapt to his feet, his metal chair hitting the floor with a clang. "Cut the bull, Nat. You guys steal whatever you can get your hands on! We got you on tape, *bro'*, red-handed." He turned to Detective Flick. "Lock him up, Sal. I got no time to waste playing games with this clown. Maybe a night in a cell with a few of his gangster homeys will soften him up." He stormed from the room.

Nate was pretty sure it was all an act, but his heart was pounding and his palms felt damp.

Detective Flick slid his chair closer, until they were sitting elbow to elbow. "Look, I'm no hothead like

Bavure. The guy has a temper like you wouldn't believe. You can tell I'm a pretty good dude, right, just a cop doing his job."

Nate nodded. He was sure he'd heard that exact line on television.

"Then try to trust me a little. Don't do this to yourself, Nate. Don't do it to your mom, your dad. I believe you, I do. But you gotta give us something on Eric, Nate, or he's going to take you down with him. Why're you protecting him? He's sure not protecting you."

The questions continued. And so did the answers. No, he wasn't aware that Eric was one of the most notorious boosters in the city. No, he didn't work with or for him. Yes, the clothes he was wearing were purchased by him. No, he didn't have the receipts with him.

During the questioning, another detective had verified that Nate was indeed a student at the Fletcher School, which no one had really disbelieved. Since he had no outstanding warrants, no criminal record, and no admission of involvement in any criminal activity, the police had no choice but to release him. Nate was given a citation for the learner's permit infraction and for a taillight violation, both punishable by payment of a fine which he could mail in. Nate didn't want to leave without Hustle, but the detectives made it clear—Eric Samson wasn't going anywhere. As Nate was leaving the precinct, a stout woman wearing a leather knapsack strode through the front door, her hair flying.

"Susan O'Graph, Legal Aid Society, for Mr. Eric Samson," she announced confidently.

The front desk cop groaned, which Nate figured was probably a good sign. He left feeling exhausted and relieved and barely made it to Grand Central Terminal in time for the last train to Edessa Hills.

10

Hi, you've found me. Leave a message after the beep and I'll find you.

"Hey Willa, it's me, Nathaniel. I'm on the train. You awake? If you're there, pick up. I really want to talk to you tonight. You there?"

Willa fixed her eyes on the telephone as if she were looking at a face.

"Aren't you gonna answer, Will?" said Jeannette, jumping up from her chair and rushing towards the phone.

"Leave it!" shouted Willa from the table where she was leaning over a Scrabble game. She studied her smooth wooden letters, carefully selected a few, and placed them one at a time on the board in a long vertical line. She whispered to herself, "Double letter on the

Q, that's twenty, plus one, two, three, four, plus ten, that's thirty-four . . . Triple word . . . that's . . . look, J, a hundred and two points!"

Jeannette dashed back to the table. "No! You are so damn competitive. Why can't you just play for word beauty instead of double this and triple that. Where's your word?"

Willa pointed proudly. "Quartz, my dear, quartz."

Jeannette moaned. "Now I really wish you'd taken Nathaniel's call. What are we playing for again?" She squinted at her letters.

"A foot rub. You might as well get started." Willa pulled off her socks, a big smile on her face.

Willa's commanding lead ensured victory and a full foot massage, so she allowed herself the luxury of chatting.

"So you know why I made him leave a message? Because his name's Schoolie back home and Nathaniel here."

From the moment a very pissed-off Willa Matthews returned to school, she and Jeannette had been discussing Willa's trip to Harlem. Not only was Willa not ever going out with Nathaniel again, but she was never going to speak to him. He was either a phony at school or a phony at home—she didn't know which version was the real one. His friends at school had their flaws but were basically nice guys on their way to college who were surely going to make something of themselves. But the guys he hung out with in Harlem, his so-called friends from childhood, had ridiculous names and were probably high school dropouts. The one she met at the Apollo was the kind of ignorant, crotch-grabbing thug her father loved to lock up. He'd been totally rude, and when she complained, Nathaniel had the nerve to take his *homeboy's* side.

"I understand how you feel," said Jeannette. "The projects are full of boys like that, so tough, so gangsta, so nowhere, and so living at home with Mama. They eyeball a girl like she's a fried bologna sandwich. It *can* be so tired, but that's all they know. Half the time they don't have fathers and their only role models are rappers and sports stars. Imagine if you were a guy and your romance teachers were that wife beater from the Wu Tang Clan and O. J. Simpson! Any girls you *did* get, if they even survived to tell the tale, would probably be over your tired butt *so fast*. What I'm saying is, they can't hold us, so they just wanna roll us."

"MC Jeannette . . ." Willa paused with her head cocked to one side. "I am *so* not moved. These homeboys spend their whole life living at home being boys. Get it? Home boys. I mean, they're not even man enough to show a girl a little respect."

"R-E-S-P-E-C-T! Find out what it means to me!"

Willa put her fingers to her ears. "Please do *not* sing that song!"

"What you got against Aretha?"

"Nothing. Just sing 'Natural Woman' or one of her other hits. In fact, never mind, don't sing at all." She slid Jeannette's newly formed word off the board. "And 'homer' is not a word. It's 'home run.' "

Jeannette shook her head. "HELLOOO? Are you American? Have you ever been to a baseball game? Homer is so a word." She could accept a legitimate loss, but Willa was not going to deprive her of the few points she could get.

"Is not, J. It's slang."

"All right, Her Willfulness. If you challenge me and the dictionary says it's a good word, you lose your turn. And since when is slang not acceptable in Scrabble?"

Willa opened the thick book and flipped to the H's. "Oh. Oops."

"Yeah, oops indeed! Oops upside ya *head*. Now I get to go twice. I feel the tide *turnin'* baby. Beware of my undertow!"

Willa laughed.

Jeannette shook her head. "You're too hard on people, you know. Anyway, Nathaniel's okay, it's not as if he dissed you—his friend did. You should give him a break. At least he wants to talk about it. Most guys would be like, Next!"

"So! Let them all move on. All I know is, my parents didn't raise me to be a hottie. I have self-respect, I go to school, any kids I have will come *after* marriage, not *to* my wedding, and I *don't* wear thongs."

"And *that's* why you got panty line!"

Willa changed the subject. She'd heard that a senior—but she didn't know who—was so paranoid about not getting accepted anywhere that she'd applied to forty colleges. And had Jeannette seen their senior ring? It was really gauche, like Wonder Woman jewelry.

They continued chatting and playing until all the letters were used. The game ended badly for Jeannette. Willa couldn't compliment her enough, she told the extravagantly sore loser, on her massage skills. Jeannette insinuated that cheating may have gone on when she went to answer the phone. After massaging Willa's feet, she made a splashy show at the sink of violently scrubbing her hands. As she was leaving, she demanded a rematch.

Nate tiptoed down the hall on the girls' floor. It was late, probably close to midnight, too late, he thought, to be doing what he was about to do. But he'd been accorded a second chance once and felt he might as well try for another. He tapped on Willa's door.

"Who is it?"

"Me," he whispered. Boys were officially banned from the girls' floors of the residence after ten o'clock.

"Me *who?*" Willa asked impatiently.

"It's Nate, Willa. I need to talk to you."

A very long minute passed before the door was unlocked and opened slightly. Willa was in a dark wool housecoat and slippers.

"What are you doing here?" she whispered back. "You know boys aren't supposed to—"

They heard sounds, talking, footsteps.

"—Come in, hurry!" she said, pulling him by the arm. "But keep your voice down. I'm not getting in trouble for *you.*"

He could tell from the way she said "you" that she was still angry. They stood just inside the door.

"I'm really messed up . . ."

"Tell me something I don't know." She had never seen him so wrecked before, looking tired and disheveled in his sloppy, oversized clothes.

"Listen, I know I was wrong yesterday. I should've put Hustle in his place."

"And where would that be, prison?"

Nate stared into space.

"Look Nathaniel, it's really late . . ."

"It's hard when you grow up with a guy and you go different ways . . . You still feel tight with him, he's family, and like family you're stuck with him"—he slumped back against the door—"even if he's a jerk and messes with you or people you're into . . ."

"Sit down. You look like you're going to keel over."

He sat down heavily on a metal chair.

"I'm not like you, Willa. All this, this school, this town, these kinds of people—you're home here . . . I'm a visitor . . . My world is a split screen with two different movies. It's sort of like what we learned in Mc-Kruma's multiculturalism class about differences in our cultures. Acting one way might seem cool in one place and be wak in another. But it's all me and I like who I am. It's just hard to make other people like all of me instead of just the part they can relate to." He exhaled wearily. "I know I'm not making any sense."

Willa nodded as if to say that he was, but she didn't actually say it.

"See, Willa, tonight my life nearly capsized. Everything I've busted my butt for as far as getting in this school and staying in it almost whooshed over a giant waterfall. Then it hit me, the stuff that really mattered, the stuff I was praying not to lose—this school, my parents being proud, the chance I have. I promised that if the cops let me go . . ."

"Cops?!"

". . . I would never take a dumb risk like that again."

"You were *arrested?*"

"Hustle was. I was just in the proverbial wrong place at the wrong time."

She'd been standing as a reminder to Nate to keep his visit short, but now she sat on the edge of her bed. Nate fell silent. Willa spoke.

"I'm not going to pretend I understand you or your friends or Harlem or any of it. You're right, I have a whole different background. I like you but . . . It's weird, you start feeling comfortable with somebody a little, then suddenly they're like Dr. Jekyll and Mr. Hyde. I liked when you kissed me. Then all of a sudden Nathaniel was Schoolie and he let his lame friend insult me—not that I'm blaming you for him but . . . It bothered me, how you were drooling over that cheesy singer, how you talked to me on the street, how you're dressed now . . . It's just really complicated, *you're* complicated. I like you, though, I do. Whoever you are."

Neither knew what else to say, so they stood and said nothing. She walked him to the door.

"See ya, Willa. Thanks for letting me in."

"See ya."

Then she startled them both. She kissed him.

The winter final exams season hit. Blustery storms left waist-high snowdrifts across the region. Horses were kept in their stables to stamp around and eat hay. Workers riding plows and blowers carved paths between walls of snow. A squat snowman wearing a Hawaiian lei stood at the school's entrance gate next to snow-covered bushes.

A few pieces of mail sat on Nate's desk. He flipped through credit card company invitations, ski trip package deals, and student insurance offers. He tore open a thin letter with no return address.

Wassup Schoolie? You probly shock to get a letter from your dawg right? I'm on lockdown charged on all kinda lacenies and robberies and thieft. Waitin for

*when they hit me with smokin' Tupac and Biggie since
they blaming me for every crime that ever happen. Been
thinking about stuff I been into, how I gotta get a
handle cause when you in the joint all you want to do is
get out and never come back. Anything can and do
happen to a brother in here. I'm cool though, got some
boys in here—they got my back. Like you did at the
precink. (You my boy 4 life!) The brotherhood taking
care of block business without me for now. My trial date
come up on the sixth. I probly gonna walk, they got
squat for proof. Gotta find me something else to do
though cause this ain't worth it.*

Holla. And remember, don't knock da Hustle!

Nate slipped the note in a large manila folder marked
"Family Mail." Before he did another thing, he got out
his pad and wrote Eric back.

It was Saturday but it felt more like a school day than
the weekend. Nate and Spencer had spent the morning
testing each other's recollection of mathematics formu-
las, French pronouns, and theories of adolescent development. Now they were keen on having some fun, and
what better way than Spencer's favorite winter activity,
skiing.

Nate grasped the poles, and slid his skis back and
forth.

"These things are sticking in the snow, Spencer. On TV the guys are speeding along. I feel like a moon walker in snowshoes."

"Is the whining going to stay at forte or are you eventually going to wind down to a soft adagio? Cross-country skis are different, and you go slower than in downhill. It's good for our quads. Once we get some momentum, we should get a good glide going. You waxed yours up good, right? Then off we go in our winter wonderland!"

They took long strides, the one bundled in red ski pants and jacket and the other in green, stabbing the frozen ground with the points of their poles to shove themselves forward. The pink of the afternoon sun spread across the snowy white landscape like a paint spill. They crossed open stretches, strained up curved slopes, and coasted down smooth hills, their muscles and lungs exulting. Neither had a sense of time passing. When they reached the very edge of the campus, they were flushed.

"Let's go in there," said Spencer, wiping his brow with a red plaid kerchief.

The old movie theater that had shut down because it simply couldn't compete against the DVDs, VCRs, and satellite dishes of Fletcher's technology-rich students had been remade into a diner called The Paunch. That's where Nate and Spencer stopped.

"Whew!" exclaimed Nate. "What a workout."

"And just think, we have to turn around and go all the way back." A woman appeared, holding a half pencil and a pad.

"I'll take the Woodsman's Special and a jumbo Coke."

"Me too," said Nate, "with a hot apple cider."

"Good idea. Forget the Coke, give me a hot apple cider too."

Spencer rubbed his hands together, blowing on them. "Hand. *Le* or *la*?"

"What?" asked Nate.

"Hand. *Le* or *la*? *Le main* or *la main*?"

"Man, forget it. I'm here to eat, not do French. I'm maxed out. *La*. Now don't bug me."

"*Très bien.* Oh, I wanted to ask you something. The holidays are bearing down upon us, Santa's on his way. I was thinking, we're buddies, we live in Manhattan, why not get together over the break? You could check out my digs, I could check out yours. It might be fun, a sort of cultural exchange program."

Spencer and Nate had slowly built a real friendship that went beyond Fletcher's mentor program. When Nate told him what had happened when *he* was stopped driving with only a permit, Spencer was genuinely angry. After that, things were changed between them, a different connection grew.

"Sure, why not? You need some real culture. And I've

always wanted to see the Central Park fountain from the thirtieth floor."

The waitress returned with plates of steak, scrambled eggs with cheese, home fries, rolls, and two steaming mugs. Nate held his face over his plate and inhaled. Spencer licked his lips. On the jukebox Faith Hill was belting out a love song. They devoured their food and then ordered hot apple pie à la mode.

"Have you seen the video for this song? She is so hot!"

Nate said the sultry country singer wasn't his type.

Spencer looked at Nate as if he'd said Dr. McKruma was a fox.

"Not your type? Faith Hill isn't a type, she's a goddess. So what *is* your type?"

Nate chuckled. "Oh I'd say about five-seven, athletic, super smart, funny . . . uh . . . what else? . . . with magic eyes and a hell of a cross-field pass."

"Willa! I *thought* my lust detector picked up a signal at that Thanksgiving dinner. She's a catch, no doubt about it, but isn't she . . . how shall we say . . . uptight? Armond said he tried and almost got shoved down a flight of stairs. He said she's seriously cryogenic."

"That's because Armond is seriously lame. Will's great."

"Will? So we're dropping syllables now? *Very* intimate. So tell me . . . what's she like, you know. With that body, she must—"

"Hey come on, Spencer! She's a nice girl and I like her a lot. We go out sometimes, that's all. We don't have to go *there*."

"So you mean you two didn't—"

"We didn't, no . . . She's not about that. And it's cool. The way things are out there, you don't want someone who's running around all over the place."

"But wait a minute, you *have* a girlfriend! You told me about her, Shondy . . . Shanti . . . and you two definitely—"

"Yeah, well I want something different now. We were only dating off and on anyway. It wasn't serious."

He hadn't told anyone but Randall about Eli and Shantay, not even his parents, and wished he could erase it from his memory. Shantay had left him a message days later making excuses, saying she'd been missing him and Eli kinda reminded her of him and they wasn't married no way and he probably had girls at school so . . . Nate never called her back. Eli hadn't bothered calling Nate at all. But then he never did anyway.

Nate looked out the window. "We better hit those hills before it gets too dark."

With the help of a strong wind at their backs, the trip home was an easy glide.

The phone rang, awakening Nate from a deep sleep. The previous day's mental and physical activities had worn him out in a way he liked. He slowly fought his way to consciousness.

"Huh? . . ." His voice was thick and dazed.

"Nate, wake up. It's your father, Nate!"

"Hello? . . . Dad? . . ." His eyes were still closed. "Somethin' happen? What happened? Mom okay?"

"Yeah, she's fine. It's Eli. Some guys beat him up pretty bad and dumped him on our block. We're at Harlem Hospital."

Nate's eyes snapped open.

"*Dumped* him . . . Is he . . . He's not . . . ?"

"No, no, no, he's alive. Hurt though, real hurt. Fractured jaw, cracked ribs, a broke hand . . . He musta made somebody real mad."

"Dammit. What happened?! Who . . . ?"

"They say he's mixed up with the numbers, been stepping on some big toes, trashed a numbers spot a while back . . . You know your brother, there's always something. Your friends from the block . . . that Brotherhood gang . . . chased the car but couldn't get the license plate number."

Nate had been pacing until he heard "trashed a numbers spot." The words froze him in his tracks.

"I'm coming home."

"No, Nate, he'll be okay. You stay up at school."

"I'm coming."

Nate rescheduled his exams. Willa asked him to call if he got a chance, let her know what was going on. The family was meeting at Eli's hospital room. When Nate descended from the train at Grand Central Terminal, he had on his school clothes. He wore them on the subway. He still had them on when he walked into the hospital, headed to room 351.

Mrs. Whitely grabbed Nate as if to say one son was hurt and she damn well wasn't going to let anything happen to the other one. Her eyelids were swollen.

"Baby!"

"Ma."

They hugged for a long time.

"Hey, Dad."

"Nate." Mr. Whitely had dark circles under his eyes. They hugged too.

"So . . ." Nate wanted to be prepared before he went in the room. "How's he doing?"

"Better," said Mrs. Whitely. "At least you can see his

eyes now. They was all swoll up . . ." Her husband took her hand.

"Go on in, son. We've been hovering over him like a pair of seagulls since last night. He said he wants some time alone with you."

There were three patients in the room, all behind curtains. Nate peeked in one and was met with a scowl from an old man with an IV tube in his arm. He looked through a split in another curtain and saw his brother. Eli was also hooked up to an IV. His head was bandaged, his eyes oozing slits, his face puffy and discolored. A short cast was fitted on his right hand.

"Eli."

Eli turned his head very slowly until he had Nate in his line of vision. "Nate . . ."

"Man, look at you . . . What happened?"

"These hoods yoked me while I was taking a few bets up in their neighborhood. Snatched me into some spot they said I wrecked and put a wrecking on me. Come to find out later, ya boy Hustle pulled that job and got busted for it. Them yokels was up on that, somebody saw him run out and jump in a Jeep. They just used that as an excuse 'cause I was taking their business."

The conversation fell silent. Nate had on his mind a topic completely unrelated to Eli's medical condition. He searched his heart, struggled to get past anger and pain, for the words that erase, cancel, delete. But words don't do those things.

Eli cleared his throat. "I screwed up; that's what I was born for I guess. You blow up, I screw up."

There was nothing Nate could do but listen. He couldn't feel the anger he'd stored away for the moment when he saw Eli again, nor could he feel love for the man in the bed, bruised and bloated as a fallen fruit.

"I was cool, doing okay. Then you showed up and took my shine. I got jealous and stayed that way. And when I had a chance, I took something from you. I'm sorry, man. You know how that is."

"No I don't, Eli. I *don't* know how that is. We're brothers yeah, but half the time it doesn't feel like we're family at all. I think the only family you have is you. You don't have any feeling for me, for Mom and Dad, not even for Shantay . . . It's all about you."

Eli tried to shake his head in disagreement but couldn't move his neck. "That ain't true, Nate. I have *much* love for y'all . . . The thing with your girl . . ."

Nate bristled. "She's not my girl. Not anymore. I *have* a girl. She's coming for Christmas." He shot a look of warning at his brother but didn't put words to it.

"Ah-ight, I hear you . . . Anyway, the thing with Shantay, that was just—"

"Spare me, Eli." Nate moved towards the curtain.

Eli shifted his body to face his brother, managing at the same time to inflict more pain on himself. He groaned.

"Stop squirming. Your tubes are gonna come out."

"Nate, man, you gotta understand."

"Understand *what?*"

"Say if Moms had another kid, a boy, and he grew up real smart like you, only smarter, and did everything right all the time and was, I don't know, like the sun in the sky, and you was just a lamp, or a flashlight."

Nate didn't know *what* his brother was talking about.

"Don't make that face, man. What I'm sayin' is, that's what it was like with me and you. I wasn't perfect, you know, no big genius or nothing like that, but I was okay. Then you came on the set and I was like, shadowed over—over and out. You know what I'm sayin'?" He groaned again, even though he hadn't moved.

Nate did know, but he was too angry to give Eli even that much.

"No."

"Come on, how you think *you* would feel, blotted out like that? Messed up. So I was like, that's cool, I do my own thing. Except I don't have no *thing* to do, so I just started hanging and slanging. Getting cash however I could. I hate working on cars and I ain't no good at it anyway. I see how Moms looks at me, all disappointed. I pick up Pop's vibe. And it only get worse when you come around, College Boy. They right, I can't compare to you."

"Why're you saying all this, Eli? So I'll feel sorry for you? Because I don't. You could've stayed in school, worked harder . . . I was even going to help you, but you didn't want help. You were too cool, too dope. Go back to school if it bothers you that much. Get a legit job and help pay some bills. Do *something* besides giving them stress."

"Nah, it's not even *about* you feeling sorry. If I was you, I wouldn't have no feeling for me either. I'm just trying to . . . apologize . . . for Shantay. I couldn't be what you are, so I wanted to take what you had . . . your girl. It wasn't her fault, she just a kid. I did it. So I'm sorry, what can I say. That was a messed up thing for a brother to do." Eli rested his hand on Nate's arm. "Sorry."

"Like I already told you, you're still my brother. That's bond. But you gotta do us better than this."

"Ah-ight, my man," they said at the same time.

Chubby Santas adorned the windows, and stockings of soft red felt hung on the walls, each one glittering with the name of a SOAR program graduate who'd made it to college. The group's annual holiday party was about to begin. To make himself heard above the scraping chairs and chatting voices, Randall cupped his hands around his mouth.

"People! People! Will everybody take his or her seat. Does anyone *not* have a handout about SOAR?"

A few kids held up their hands. Volunteers passed flyers to them.

The large turnout was impressive, but that meant little. The flyers distributed in the schools trumpeted "A SOAR Party for Students of All Ages! Food, Beverages, Dancing, and Gifts!"—an offer few resisted. If twenty-five kids showed up, maybe five actually filled out a form for further information.

"Most of you," said Randall, "are probably hearing about the program for the first time, some already know about it, and a few came for the free food."

Kids laughed and pointed at each other.

"That would be Lakita over here!"

"Ya *mama* want free food! I came here to sign up for college!"

"No matter," Randall went on, raising both hands for quiet, "as long as you're here. I'll just go over the basics about SOAR." He explained how the program worked and the criteria for selection, adding that it wasn't about signing up but rather qualifying through tests for a private school that prepared students for college.

"Why everything gotta be about a tess? I always do bad on tesses, but that don't mean I'm dumb."

"Yes it *do*!"

More laughter. Randall was used to the rowdy scene, which was repeated every year. And it was always the kids who had indeed come only for the free food who made the most noise. Few had ever set foot on the Columbia campus, although many lived nearby.

"*You* dumb. That's why ya hat on backward. To fit over ya backward brain."

Nate was fidgeting in his chair. It wasn't as if he

hadn't talked in front of people before. He did well in his presentations at Fletcher. But that was school, and those kids were preppies. This was New York, and these were his peers. What really had Nate's stomach in a knot though was Willa, standing near the windows at a table covered with pamphlets and brochures. Next to her stood Jeannette. Each girl was wearing a stick-on tag with her name and "Student Volunteer" written on it. Why didn't Randall get someone else to speak; why *him*? *Because*, Randall said, boys think school is for girls, so they need to hear from a boy who likes school.

"Okay, settle down, folks! May I have your attention *please*. I'd like to introduce to you . . ."

"I'm hungry!"

". . . a graduate of SOAR who hails from right here in Harlem, USA . . ."

"Big up Harlem!"

"Big up *Broooonnx*!"

"Brooklyn in the *house*!"

"Brooklyn in the *out*house!"

"The *dog*house!"

Choking back a chuckle, Randall adopted his stern voice. "C'mon guys, let's show each other a little respect. There will be no music, no prizes—and definitely no food—until our guest has had a chance to speak, so it's up to you."

Things quieted down.

"Our speaker goes to a top prep school and is on his way to college, just like some of you may be one day. I am proud to present to you Harlem's own Nathaniel Whitely!"

"Whitey?!"

"Hardly!"

"Blackly!"

Willa and Jeannette began clapping. Nate felt a rush of pride as he stood. Others joined indifferently, willing to do anything with their hands until they were finally holding food. He smiled and coughed. A couple of boys checking out Nate's FUBU sneakers nodded with approval. A girl yelled that his Projectboy jeans were "smokin'." Looking at the faces in the room, he saw his neighbors, his family, himself. And it was definitely all good. He hadn't written down anything to say, figuring he'd just talk. He began by describing the street he grew up on, his crew of solid friends, his folks' encouragement, his brother's endless dramas. Some kids shook their heads, as if they too had wak brothers. The Brotherhood protected his block, he said, and school gave him the chance to check out what was beyond that block. Here he looked at Willa, who immediately took an elbow in her side from Jeannette. College lets you choose your own future, Nate said, instead of getting tripped up and trapped down by street-thug madness that just lands you in jail. His main man was on lockdown because he didn't give himself enough choices, and that was a shame.

That's where Nate ended the speech. And that's when a voice rang out from the back of the room.

"I'm out, Schoolie! I got probation!"

Nate stared for a moment at Hustle, grinning in a Ghetto Fabwear white leather bomber and black leather jeans. Then he cracked up laughing. Within an instant, there was no one in the room who wasn't laughing. Hustle made his way to the front, greeting familiar faces from the neighborhood. The boys grasped hands and slapped each other on the back. Applause filled the room.

"You just *had* to steal my spotlight!"

"Hell yeah, dawg," said Hustle, scanning the room. "Too many cuties up in here for them to be only looking at *you*." He winked at Jeannette, who rolled her eyes hard.

Randall rose and quickly thanked Nathaniel, the SOAR board of directors, and Columbia University. He invited anyone with questions to grab him or Nathaniel or any of the student volunteers.

"Now, let's party!" he said, and turned on the music.

———

Nate and Hustle pulled up chairs and joined Willa and Jeannette at the information table. Nate was excited to see his friend.

"It's so good to see you. How long have you been out, and why didn't you give me a shout? You know you're like a brother to me!"

"All the way, Schoolie," responded Hustle. He lowered his voice. "On the *brother* tip, I heard about Eli when I was in the joint. He okay?"

"Yeah, I think. He's working with my dad again. I just hope it lasts. But what happened with you and the case and everything?"

"Oh man, you know how they play it, making folks go back and forth to court till they break down. I had enough and just took a plea so I could get off with probation . . ." He looked at Jeannette. "Even though I'm innocent."

Jeannette half smiled.

"I'm fresh out the yard and back on the streets. Your moms told me where to find you. All I have to do is stay cool . . . find some *other* kind of gainful employment." A look of worry flashed across his face. He turned towards Willa and quickly changed the subject. "And how *you* be, Miss Willa Fine-as-Always?"

"Fine as always," she said, trying not to sound cold, which is exactly how she sounded.

"My man Nate gots to be the luckiest brother there is, bagging a *classy* hottie like . . ."

Willa did *not* try to hide her frown. "Don't they have English classes for prisoners up where you—"

Nate jumped in like a referee between two tangled boxers. "I bet Randall can help you out, Hustle. He knows everybody and is hooked up with all kinds of training programs. You should get his card."

Hustle had already directed his attention elsewhere. Nate followed his gaze.

"I'm so blown away," said Nate, laughing, "that I forgot to introduce you guys. Jeannette, Hustle. Hustle, Jeannette."

"Wassup, shorty," said Hustle.

"Shorty? Whatever. I'm taller than you."

Willa laughed. She could tell when Jeannette liked a boy. Jeannette liked Hustle.

Hustle leaned back so he could see under the table. "Them legs *do* look kinda long. But that's ah-ight, I ain't scared."

The four of them hung out together, eating and dancing. Lots of girls and a few guys approached Nate with questions. Willa reluctantly danced with Hustle to give Jeannette a break and, despite her best efforts, couldn't help but laugh at his funny comments. One on one, she decided, he was a little less obnoxious. Jeannette recognized in him so many boys she'd grown up around and saw past his hoodlum facade. Randall was pleased by the number of kids actually interested in the SOAR program and was already making plans to get Nate back the following year, maybe even have him visit schools.

The party wound down, donated gifts were distributed, and the volunteers cleaned up. Hustle suggested they take in a movie "down at Forty-deuce."

"Maybe you should stay away from Forty-deuce for a while," said Nate, winking.

"I hate that atmosphere," protested Willa. "It's still so seedy, even though it's supposed to be cleaned up. What about something right around here? I like Columbia."

Jeannette sucked her teeth. "Manhattan isn't the *only* borough of New York, you know. Brooklyn has movies too. There's a big multiplex near where I live and it costs less than here."

The ensuing silence made Jeannette suck her teeth again.

"Y'all stuck-up."

The Magic Johnson movie theaters on 125th won and they got their coats. Randall congratulated Nate on his inspiring talk, thanked Willa and Jeannette for their help, and praised Hustle for his dramatic entrance, which everyone had loved. As they were all heading for the door, Hustle turned around, rushed over to Randall, and returned waving the architect's business card.

"Hey, ya never know what the future holds."

Each of them considered that thought as they walked across the wintry campus and headed uptown.